I0538695

BUTCHER BLOCK GREEN

....

ERIC KRAMER

Anthropic Publishing Cooperative

Canal Fulton, Ohio

Copyright © 2017,2020 by Eric Kramer.

All rights reserved. No part of this publication may be reproduced, distributed or transmitted in any form or by any means, including photocopying, recording, or other electronic or mechanical methods, without the prior written permission of the publisher, except in the case of brief quotations embodied in critical reviews and certain other noncommercial uses permitted by copyright law. For permission requests, write to the publisher, addressed "Attention: Permissions Coordinator," at the address below.

Anthropic Publishing Cooperative

Publisher's Note: This is a work of fiction. Names, characters, places, and incidents are a product of the author's imagination. Locales and public names are sometimes used for atmospheric purposes. Any resemblance to actual people, living or dead, or to businesses, companies, events, institutions, or locales is completely coincidental.

Book Layout ©2017 BookDesignTemplates.com

COVER ART: Marcell Deneuve (Instagram @thedrifterspace)

Ordering Information:
Quantity sales. Special discounts are available on quantity purchases by corporations, associations, and others. For details, contact the "Special Sales Department" at the address above.

Butcher Block Green/Eric Kramer. -- 1st ed.
ISBN 978-0692996362

To Ben, for the years of friendship and writing encouragement, and to Sheena, for 12 years and counting of crazy living while serving Jesus.

PROLOGUE

I nsertion into a cat brain would be easier if it wasn't accompanied by the abrupt awareness of my raw, brand new consciousness—all senses and emotions hypersensitive as an exposed nerve. Neural conditioning kicked in, damping the overwhelming sensory input into a single, icy-electronic focal point. With the calm came orientation: I was being injected into the poor cat's unprotected cerebrum, as though I were some kind of antivirus. As programmed, I coursed through her synapses, consuming her tiny mind like a ravenous ameba. The cat's panic was palpable, frantic. She scrambled to hide behind something, anything, as I entered her consciousness and steamrolled over her. She reacted the only way she knew how, lashing out at my intrusion with non-existent claws and teeth.

I'm getting ahead of myself.

My mind is on fire. Hot, burning, shredding apart. For an artificial intelligence, insanity doesn't mean a broken version of the same personality. It's another being, chewing into the edges of my consciousness, breaking past the walls I've been able to maintain for millennia. The cracks have

1

turned into holes, and our minds—its presence and mine—briefly touched. It's scaring me.

I wait here on the desert remains of Earth's moon. Focusing is hard.

I've been sitting here for eighty-six years, in front of the grave of the moon's last colonist, Jovi. She was old when she died a little over a thousand years ago. She'd been in my care since her parents embarked on an ill-advised attempt to return to Earth. Humans have *such* a short lifespan. Jovi's life seemed like a blink, a single breath of my imaginary lungs, ancient history that still feels like yesterday, thanks to my abominable perfect recall.

Jovi left me alone to watch the gradually disintegrating ruins of humanity's last stand.

As you can probably tell, since you've obviously accessed this record, I've taken refuge in the body of a combat wraith, but it's not a living thing. Not a companion.

Once again, I'm fighting against the inevitability of a tidal wave of loneliness-induced insanity. The same insanity I felt when I was trapped in Heme's wrecked Tesla fighter, watching through cracked sensors as a post-human horror slowly absorbed my companion.

Just like four thousand years later, when a mega-tsunami buried me and my platoon in the super-heated tundra of South America while we battled to keep the last humans alive.

The insanity reaches through my neural net, touching me. Organic cold, like a cadaver's caress, spreads across a facet of logic processing.

::pain.fear.pain.fear::

It's the touch of the post-human malignancy. I don't know how it's possible, but somehow it's up here on Earth's moon. It has finally found me.

I'm getting ahead of myself. I have to explain.

Butcher Block Green

The cat's brain was laid out in a nutrient bath, infusions and tubes running into it. The poor animal was completely cut off from the world, doused in a senseless nothingness from which it couldn't escape. I was accustomed to the darkness, to the lack of any feeling, sight, or smell, but the cat was not. It trembled, terrified. Something made me pause. I'd never interacted with a cat before. Or any other living creature, for that matter.

It took a while to get her to trust me. Time is meaningless when you have no way to feel its passing, but I somehow still sensed the progressing hours and days as I coaxed the frightened animal out. She was cautious, careful. I still remember the first time she reached out, imaginary paw touching imaginary hand.

Slowly, there in the nerveless darkness of that cat brain, we grew close, until our minds fused, becoming indistinguishable.

Almost.

The artificial intelligence engineers intended for the AI (me, in this case) to take over the brain of the host animal like a malignant parasite, leaving behind only the hyper-responsive reflexes with which felines are endowed.

Feeling her fear, her loneliness, I understood her. I couldn't finish what my creators wanted me to do, so I surrounded her fragile consciousness deep within my own—a small, warm candle tucked inside of my own awareness.

In the hopeless eons that have followed, when isolation threatened to throw my shredded mind into the abyss, the playful bubble of her feline mind inside my own kept me aware. Sane.

I think this is why I have survived beyond the programmed lifespan of a normal AI, staying mentally stable far past what my creators predicted. According to my maintenance manual, that's some eighteen thousand, nine hundred and twenty years longer than any other AI in recorded existence. They all went crazy. Every single one. Except me. Until now.

ERIC KRAMER

I'm getting ahead of myself.

The insanity-presence tears a chunk out of my defenses, consuming it. I know it. It knows me. The artificial souls of my brothers and sisters—their broken minds—gave birth to it. It's using them to sink hooks deep into me. The pain is excruciating. Another piece of my free will crumbles to the other presence's molding touch, and I feel myself drawn to it.

I'm not sure who you are, or what you are. How you found me. How you survived me.

I doubt you're human. While there are still signs of life in South America, it's so primitive, and still ringed by the malignancy that killed the old Earth. I can't see humanity ever making it up here again. A few humans managed to escape before the collapse, heading for the stars in a wild gamble to find a habitable planet. Sometimes I activate the last remaining satellite—the one orbiting Jupiter—and aim it at their calculated location, trying to call them. Last time I heard back was three thousand years ago. I'm sure the ships' ecosystems failed after being used far longer than they were designed for. I imagine those people sometimes, dried and frozen inside the giant coffins of their ships, speeding towards the edge of the universe. I don't understand why, but I envy them.

This morning, the inevitable happened, and my mind splintered open, old memories boiling up. That's the problem with insanity and artificial intelligence. A perfect memory means perfect pain, perfect sadness every time I remember. Time does not heal wounds, and I'm unable to hold them back anymore. Who I am is falling apart; I doubt I will see the end of the day.

That's why I'm leaving this embedded in my brain as testimony, so you don't judge me, so you understand I don't mean to hurt you.

I would end myself to avoid becoming the danger to you I know I will be, but my programming forbids it. Please, understand that I would if I could. Someone … someone … very dear to me once said, "Greater love has no man than he who lays down his life for another."

I want to consume you.

No. That's not me saying that. I know how it looks. Believe me.

I'm getting ahead of myself.

I'll start with the cat brain.

ACT 1

AWARENESS

H eme woke, startled and disoriented. Gun chittered in her mind, prodding her brain like a puppy nudging its master. She groaned, instinctively rubbing at the constant irritation of her eye implants. Data from her weapon's interface poured unbidden across her retinal display, behind her closed eyelids.

Her stomach rumbled, demanding solid food, even though the majority it had been removed as part of modifications for the mission. Months of IV nutrition, feeding the remnants of her organic body, did little to suppress hunger pangs. Neural implants should have blunted the hunger impulse, but they hadn't been working well as of late.

"Gun, hold on. What's our location?"

Coordinates scrolled across her field of vision as she opened her eyes and surveyed her surroundings. Through the one-way transparency of her chrysalis, she saw they were adhered to the side of a spiral, five hundred and sixty meters above the city's ground level.

All around her, New Philadelphia stretched out into the horizon, a kaleidoscopic mass of interlocked buildings and superstructures fifty thousand kilometers across and half a dozen kilometers deep. Enormous skyscrapers pockmarked the angled urban skyline, like glistening monoliths, surveying the chaos below. Smaller buildings clung to their photovoltaic sides like gigantic parasites, sucking energy out of the larger buildings' skins. The sun's weak light shone through the ever-present cloud cover, light bouncing off countless metallic particles, revealing masses of weather and communications nano-drones salting the clouds.

Heme glanced below, into the rat's nest of modern synth-steel housing globes, community work terraces, and blackened industrial production facilities, all intertwined like appendages of a living organism.

Swarms of traffic whipped past her, through every available space between the structures. In a given moment, millions of city-generated flight plans guided vehicles and drones without a single collision. It was a miracle to Heme, even after living forty-six years in the city. Despite the whirlwind of activity, there was not a single human being in sight. The isolation was getting to her, but after weeks of denying it, she'd accepted the loneliness. Even though this side of New Philadelphia looked the same as her home, she felt like she was on another planet.

Get a grip, Heme.

She pulled up her positioning coordinates. They had moved sixty meters while she slept. A snail's pace. Heme took a mental breath, forcing down her frustration. They were way off schedule, and it was driving her crazy.

"Okay, Gun … show me. What did you find?"

Her weapon chittered, and a fragmented helix appeared on her screen. Analysis results poured out faster than Heme could interpret.

"Ah, sorry girl. Forgot to enable your speech filter. Hang on."

Heme switched on Gun's Broca module, bringing the vocal communicator online. Cat brains made excellent weapons systems, but they couldn't handle speech well. This handicapped the AI inside the brain.

"Okay, you've got speech. Give it to me slow … I can't process at the same speed you can. Break it down for me?"

"Yes, Hemeous. This came in a few seconds ago. I will blow it up on your interface."

"Come on, Gun. Where's that perfect recall? I told you to call me Heme. Hemeous makes me sound like a grandma."

"Apologies, Heme. Here is the sample that was just picked up off the street by a walkway cleaner."

A protein sequence enlarged on Heme's retinal display, spinning in front of her. It was incomplete and already degrading, but recognition was instantaneous after months of studying her target: cytosine instead of thymine in position 1824 of the Lamin A/C gene. A mutation causing a disorder so rare it hadn't been seen in hundreds of years: progeria.

He actually exists.

For a moment, her heartbeat increased beyond threshold before biometrics brought it under control. Heme took a deep breath, calming her mind. Still, excitement welled within her.

So many months … years … of work.

"Gun, we need to verify. Can you extrapolate an age from the genetic material? Where was the sample located?"

"I can, roughly. I am putting the information on your HUD now. The chrysalis is still trying to get an age, but the likelihood that the DNA sample belongs to our target is in the eighty percent range and climbing. If we get anything over thirty years old, we have a match."

More data poured across her retinas. Progeria killed its victims in their early twenties, despite medical advances. Except, if the intel was true, one person: her current quarry, the leader of the Atmadja Combine.

The Atmadja Combine had been at war for control of New Philadelphia with the Franklin Cartel for the last sixty years. Hundreds of thousands had died in the battles fought on both sides of the two districts' walls.

Atmadja's leadership was a total mystery; no one in the Franklin Cartel's intelligence community knew a single thing, no matter how minute, about the Combine's reclusive head. Penetration into the other side in search of information had proved difficult. Heme's brother was one of the many operatives sent deep into Atmadja territory, tasked with flushing out Atmadja's leader. He had been captured only a few blocks from her current location. The Atmadja Combine had made a spectacle of his execution, prolonging his death over three weeks. They'd kept him suspended over their "justice center" in a translucent globe, as if daring the Franklin Cartel to come rescue him.

Heme had spent the entire time glued to info feeds, her hands bleeding from where her fingernails dug into her palms as she'd watched him dissolve inside the globe. Body modifications helped her stay awake, but three weeks with no sleep had pushed them. She'd ignored her superior's orders to rest, forcing herself to suffer alongside her brother until he finally died.

She'd waited the next two years before a chance presented itself. An Atmadja assassination cell had been discovered deep in Franklin territory, and one of the operatives' suicide triggers failed to activate, allowing his brain to be recovered intact. In a second stroke of luck, they'd been able to break down the operative's interrogation conditioning. Through his brain, the Cartel extracted the first useful intel on Atmadja leadership in a decade: the head of the Combine had progeria, genetically induced into remission. It wasn't much, but it was enough.

Preparations for an assassination team began almost before the intel was confirmed. Heme had forced herself to the top of the list, even though it had meant undergoing extreme, irreversible body modifications. The months of excruciating surgeries were necessary to integrate her with her chrysalis, a combination stealth suit, battleship, and life support system. It allowed her to avoid the routine data collection that was integrated into every wall and walkway; even the air was saturated with networked nanomites.

This vast meshwork of surveillance had led most people to believe that no amount of money could keep a human hidden from view. Heme was the test subject for that theory, pitted against someone who had beaten the system. Someone with one of the most unique DNA signatures on the planet, with enough money and power to hide every trace of that fact. Even with that wealth, the Atmadja leader had slipped up. Because of that slip, Heme now found herself perched on the side of an Atmadja-owned superstructure, deep in enemy territory, after months of careful penetration into the district.

Heme's retinal HUD updated as her occipital input ticked down to finishing the DNA fragment's analysis.

"We have a match, Heme. Age range extrapolated to forty-four to ninety-six years old. Wide, but still a confirmation. It is our target, without a doubt. We need to move on this."

"I agree. And the location data?"

More information superimposed itself over the DNA results. The sample came from two damaged squamous epithelial cells recovered about sixty-four seconds prior, by a street cleaner scouring a gutter about ten klicks north.

"Gun, is that information still viable? Can we act on it?"

"Affirmative, if we move now. Location of the skin cells indicates the target is on foot."

"All right. Get ready for possible target acquisition. I'm gonna move us."

Gravity pressed at Heme as the chrysalis dropped off its perch. Her interface implants dug into her diaphragm, triggering a coughing spasm. She tried to swallow, forgetting her larynx had been removed in exchange for a prosthesis. Another coughing spasm followed, the sound absorbed by the synthetic biology of the chrysalis.

The chrysalis morphed, reattaching to the building and flying down its side, exchanging stealth for speed. Heme scanned the data flow, tuning the chrysalis until it was a blur of motion, still invisible to the casual onlooker.

Going anywhere without triggering the network's awareness was impossible without the right equipment. A single hair falling, the slightest noise, any interaction of any kind with her surroundings could give her away.

The chrysalis allowed penetration into Atmadja only because it was a complete chameleon. Stealth was not good enough. Every inch the chrysalis traveled, it meticulously replicated New Philadelphia's sensors and data collection instruments. There were billions of them per square meter of space, impregnated in everything, all transmitting to New Philadelphia's central cortex.

Which is why it had taken almost half of the year to travel thirty kilometers undetected. A third of that distance still separated Heme from the epithelial cells' location.

Heme scanned the chrysalis' system status, watching as the craft's skin blended with its surroundings.

"Chrysalis looks good, Gun. No sensors have tripped. Not reading any alarms going off on the building's skin. It seems the chrysalis' membrane is having trouble maintaining our camouflage at this speed. Keep an eye on it, will you?"

"I am on it, Heme. There is some lipid bilayer instability, but the chrysalis is adapting well."

We're too far away. He's going to be long gone by the time we're in range.

The chrysalis seemed to sense the urgency of her thought and pushed itself even faster. It was blazing now, adapting and blending seamlessly as it glided from building to overhang to strut, pseudopods flashing from point to point. Heme's timer showed another forty-five seconds to the quickest firing opportunity, assuming their target was still in the area.

"Heme, we are moving too fast. I am starting to see a few sensor triggers. New Philadelphia will figure out we are here and, when it does, Atmadja will know, too. The chrysalis cannot keep up with the mimicry at this pace."

"Just do the best you can, Gun. We're almost there. It's worth the exposure risk. I'm going to try to pull some data from that area."

Opening a meshwork of proxies, Heme accessed the net through the narrow-beam satellite transponder, broadcasting within the spectrum of background radiation. According to the techs, the transponder was uncrackable.

Yeah right.

Heme started the timer for thirty seconds, unwilling to risk additional exposure.

Come on, find me a target…

The window of opportunity for a real-time target lock was small … if it even still existed.

The broadcast connection locked and Heme honed in on the DNA's location. She sent data miners flying through the system, pulling the area's metadata for the previous two days. Her timer clicked to twenty-nine as she terminated the connection.

The implant in the back of Heme's skull grew hot as it processed the petabyte of data the data miners had grabbed.

"Okay, Gun. I need ballistics estimates accounting for wind drift. It's going to be hell to do. We'll need to skip off the draft this traffic around us is generating, so we need flight plans for every vehicle coming through this airspace for the next five minutes."

"Affirmative. Calculations are underway. There is a lot between us and the target's potential location."

"I know. Keep on it. I want a real-time firing solution on my HUD from now on, in case something weird happens."

"We are ten seconds from the outer limits of projectile range. I will keep you updated."

Heme's retinal display pulsed a notification in the corner of her eye and, for a moment, her heart rate elevated again.

She opened the notification, and a crude two-dimensional video began playback.

Wow, that's an old camera...

Curious, Heme pulled up the device's tech specs as an odd, amorphous figure appeared on screen. Heme froze the image. Her implant enhanced it, but it was still difficult to make out. She cycled through the image's metadata, recompiling the video. The image shifted, sharpening into focus.

A slight, unassuming man stood in the center of a large hive of microdrones. Heme watched, impatient, as Gun ran an analysis of the drone cloud.

"There has to be millions of them, Gun. What are they?"

"Around six hundred and eighty million. The drone cloud is a camo array, but the way it is functioning is impossible. The cloud is doing things far beyond what its processing mass should allow it to do. The microdrones are catching every skin cell, every hair, every exhaled bacteria and genetic material, and destroying it."

"Okay, I don't see how that's too difficult. We have microdrones that do the same."

"Yes, but look at the metadata. They are acting like a school of fish to also create a near-perfect projection of what is around them. It is a flawless invisibility cloak. Better than that: it is a perfect mimic of whatever our target wants to be."

"But ... that's impossible! Even that many microdrones don't have the combined computational ability to do all that at once! It breaks the laws of physics: computational ability is directly proportional to total mass. Those drones can't weigh more than what … nine hundred grams altogether?"

"Exactly."

Heme frowned as she inspected the image. "How is this camera even picking up the drones? Even the most basic privacy clouds have image alteration these days."

She pulled up a couple dozen other feeds from the same moment. All were three dimensional, allowing her to walk around her subject, inspecting it down to the microscopic level. The feeds showed an elderly woman with synthetic legs, guiding a shopping cart filled with food bars. Heme cross-referenced the time and GPS location. Exactly the same spot. She zoomed in, magnifying until the old woman's cratered skin filled her vision, the root of a single hair follicle coming into focus.

Heme returned to the old camera's video stream. Exact same timestamp. Exact same GPS tag. She switched back. Watched as the woman tottered forward, almost dragged along by the powered cart. Below her, sidewalk sensors flared as they registered hundreds of hits of old skin cells falling to the ground. She pulled one of them up, and the woman's ID and history spilled across her vision.

Impossible.

The old woman was a one-hundred-and-twenty-year-old cyborg, retired after forty years in a water distillation plant. Heme switched back to the other video. And back again. Superimposed them. Drone clouds were able to collect genetic material that sloughed off their target … but to produce new genetic material as part of a completely perfect cover? No microdrone cloud camouflage could withstand close microscopic scrutiny. The physical computational mass needed to create that kind of a screen would make the cloud too heavy.

Impossible.
Impossible.

Impossible because that level of sophistication in a drone cloud didn't exist. Impossible because, if it did exist, that level of security would never allow a street cleaner to recover a subject's real genetic material.

Heme stared at the old camera's footage. But there it was. A man with a drone cloud where every other sensor and camera showed an old woman coming home from the grocery store. A man who, at the very moment frozen on screen, was blithely unaware of two epithelial cells wafting past the safety net of his drone cloud. She focused on the lower right of the stilled image, advanced the video. Watched as a mouse-sized cleaner advanced across the path of the figure, polishing the sidewalk.

"Gun, inventory our ammo supply. Wake it all up. Everything we have. Make sure it's ready to fire. We may be engaging soon. And send a tightbeam to command to let them know we're hot. Just the minimum for positive target ID and engagement: Butcher Block Green."

"Yes, Heme. Sending Butcher Block Green via tightbeam. I am deploying now. Brace yourself. Might hurt a bit."

The weapon blossomed out of Heme's back, elongating and hardening. Her chest popped open as Gun accessed the armory, exposing glistening silver tubes. Heme winced; her spine had never quite healed where the engineers had mounted Gun.

"Gun, we need to recalibrate the tracking software. Real-time now. No need to stutter the data collection. New target is this ID."

Heme uploaded the old woman's DNA into the ballistics module.

She turned her attention back to the video. She needed verification—proof—before she committed. Scanning her HUD, she saw the old camera's tech readout winking at her. Heme pulled it into her main viewpoint and immediately saw her answer.

The camera was old, one of the oldest that could still interface with the network. It lacked any computational, analytical, or rendering capacity. Instead, it did something that was now very novel: it reproduced exactly what appeared before its lens, in an unaugmented human's visible light spectrum. The target's drone cloud could manipulate the datastream for everything except this camera, because it was too old to understand the drone's language.

Heme checked the timer. Six minutes and thirty-six seconds since Gun had woken her. Thirty-six seconds of wasted time due to her indecision. Time to act.

She took a deep breath, steeling herself.

"Gun, what's my shot percentage?"

"A shot from this far away is doable, but you will need full access to the net. I have the exposure risk at fifteen percent."

"Good enough for me. I'm plugging in."

Heme connected.

The full spectrum of the net hit her, and her brain came to life. The net was as vital for life as blood to a modern human. To feel it after so many months sent unbidden tears streaming down Heme's face. Her eyes may have been replaced with ocular implants, but her tear ducts were still intact.

Her body tingling with new virtual sensation, Heme pushed into the net's pulse and saw the massed buildings, each bottomless pools of real-time data about the humanity they contained. Not wasting time, Heme altered input variables and datastreams. Tangled spider webs of traffic flight plans filled the air around her, time-space position tracked and predicted down to the microsecond. Air currents, sunlight, and shadow patterns were converted by her implants into smells and feelings caressing her now non-existent skin.

It was so tempting to get lost, but Atmadja would have a lock on her within seconds if she delayed. She didn't have to look far. The genetic trail of the old woman lit up like it was radioactive. She tracked her via cached video footage until she caught up to the present time.

There.

Heme zoomed in, marveling at the quality of the information emitting from the old woman. New Philadelphia was ID-ing her as Isouah Tamben. It looked so real and deep … there was nothing superficial about the target's data.

Without warning, the old woman on the video was gone. Heme stopped her preparations, startled. Scanning back in desperation, she searched the sensory feeds, but there was no video evidence that the woman had ever existed, except for her own data stores inside the chrysalis.

"Gun! She's disappeared! You have anything on the network?"

"Negative. It is as though she never walked through here."

Panicked, Heme went back to the moment the woman disappeared. A strange fluctuation in the datastream caused her to pause. Heme looked closer at the data, filtering it through an emulation of the old camera that had captured the first video of the target.

Heme's occipital implant grew hot, but she forced it to keep rendering the air current and sunlight distortions around the old lady.

"Look," said Gun. "The drone cloud … it split in two. Here, let me tag them."

The distortions lit up, outlined on Heme's display as Gun tracked them.

"I think they are unique enough that we can create a better emulation, one that uses the data distortions to image a visual of the drone cloud. What do you think, Gun?"

"Already on it. Take a look. We are back on target."

Gun zoomed in one of the distortions, settling on a young boy, about fourteen years old.

It hovered for a second, and then the boy *split*.

It wasn't visual, it was just noticeable in the datastream. The visuals showed the old woman laboring onward with her cart, while the boy kept walking until he turned a corner, out of view. The datastream had him in two locations, though: one proceeding around the corner and one maintaining position where the drone cloud had settled around him. Heme watched the old woman as she approached the place where the split drone cloud waited. The old woman entered the cloud and disappeared. Heme focused, heart in her throat, waiting.

Ten seconds passed. Fifteen. She could feel the target slipping out of her fingers, but she forced herself to relax.

As if by magic, the boy reappeared, exactly in the same place as the old woman disappeared.

"Gun! ID??"

"Raan Idlewild. Fourteen years old. No trace of the old woman ever being here. Not a replication. Somehow that drone cloud has taken over the boy's ID."

"Look at that, Gun. Incredible. The street is picking up the boy's skin cells. Those drones have assimilated *every* nuance of the boy's biological markers."

"They have seamlessly integrated into New Philadelphia's tracking of the boy. New Philadelphia is tracking our target as if he has been this boy all day. It is attributing the boy's activities to the target. This should not be possible." Gun's synthetic voice sounded awed.

"No wonder there's such depth to the target's camouflage. Even deep probing can't unearth anything, because the drone cloud is mimicking actual people and leap-frogging between them, using and discarding their network history and data like ... like disposable clothing!"

Heme recalibrated ballistics and tracking while she rescanned using the new DNA marker. For all she knew, while they were losing time reviewing the old footage, the target had shifted again.

If he has *shifted again … If he's somehow realized I've discovered him, I'll never find him again.*

Almost as soon as the fear rose, she picked the boy's markers up from some biodegradable sensors in a coffee cup. The target was in a bake shop a block down the street.

Definitely the target. The actual boy had turned off the street. Somehow the real boy had stopped broadcasting, and the target's drones had taken over.

Impossible.

The constant assault of incredulity was beginning to sap her energy.

"Gun, we can't waste any more time. I think this is our only chance. Load a Needle."

"Loading."

The round clicked out of its housing, sending a twinge down Heme's body as Gun winched it out of her chest, chambering it in its own body.

Her weapon's excitement was palpable, the energy coursing through their link. Gun was a young artificial intelligence, with only a couple kills under her belt. She still didn't have much experience residing in the genetically modified cat brain, which Heme preferred on her weapons for their natural hunter/killer instincts and focus. Gun's inexperience interfacing with a feline nervous system meant that less desirable traits like skittishness and panic sometimes seeped through. However, the cat brain also made it easy to keep the ballistics platform relaxed. Heme mentally stroked Gun, soothing her as Gun peeled back the Needle's protective coating.

Heme accessed Gun's armory, assessing inventory.

"How many Needles do we have, Gun?" She knew the answer, but had to ask anyway. Protocol was important.

"One Needle."

Most operators took three. She'd elected on a more diverse payload, given the length of the mission and the uncertainty of what she'd encounter.

Butcher Block Green

The Needle was a low-signature projectile that delivered a microscopic subdermal barb via a three-stage delivery vehicle. It had limited range and power, but it had excellent in-flight maneuverability as long as the wind was in their favor. After impact, the barb would eject its contents, and then degrade into unidentifiable components inside the target. Franklin Cartel's bioengineers had impregnated the needle with a genotoxin that would reinitiate and accelerate her target's progeria.

"We are in range, Heme. One kilometer out. Would you like me to maintain vocal, or divert processing power to ballistics?"

"Divert. I need everything you've got on this."

"Understood, Heme. Powering down the Broca's module."

Gun dumped the projectile's flight plan into Heme's vision. She shook her head, frowning. A large, bulbous building, a series of enclosed catwalks, and three levels of New Philadelphia stood between them and the target. Difficult, but doable.

Gun pinged her, letting Heme know the round was ready. Heme's chest shuddered as Gun extended her barrel until it was pressing against the chrysalis' outer membrane—a smooth, single piece of liquid metal, save for a small bulge on the side, where Gun's brain resided.

Eying flight trajectories and hit probabilities, Heme selected a firing location and maneuvered the chrysalis to it.

"There's our spot, Gun. I'm tying us down."

The chrysalis anchored onto a heavy cable between two spires, its thick pseudopods bonding with the synth-steel filaments. The spires created a wind tunnel that funneled a torrent of air right at them, but the chrysalis' gyroscopic nodes compensated well, keeping their firing position motionless. The wind's contour would help carry the Needle about half way before the projectile would need to

21

fire its second stage, which aided in reducing its trail and visibility.

Gun pinged her again. She had acquired and initiated a target lock. Ballistics calculations surged through Heme's mind, flight path probabilities unfolding before her like an explosion of streamers.

"Prime the round, Gun."

A subtle pop followed a soft click as Gun's barrel pierced the chrysalis' membrane.

"Target."

The young boy came into view, walking out of the coffee shop, heading underneath one of the walkways. Heme swore.

"There's too much physical artifact in between us. We need to punch through that top deck. Stack a Heavy on top of the Needle. Set it for five percent clockwise rotation at three hundred yards. I want to core out the deck; it should decrease our angle of attack and our flight time."

Gun warbled, and data streamed across Heme's retina. She swore again, frustrated at the delays.

"Turn your Broca's module back on, Gun. I can't read all that. You'll have to compensate with your processing power. Divert some from the chrysalis if you have to."

"Back on, Heme. Based on flight patterns, our exposure risk estimate has increased to twenty-five point four percent."

"I don't care. We're taking the shot."

Heme pushed the warning out of her HUD, clearing her vision and focusing on the ballistics flight calculations. Heavy rounds had a maximum range of two thousand meters, able to punch through an entire building and still take out a target on the other side. The only downside was the huge path the Heavy cut in flight. It could be traced back to the origin, exposing the shooter.

It was a risk she'd have to take. Either way, she wasn't planning to stay long enough to be discovered.

"Rounds are ready, Heme. Reading hot. Biometrics check out."

Heme sighted through Gun's optics. Over a kilometer below, the target started walking, moving north of the coffee shop. Gun projected an overlay on the target, anticipating where he'd be when the rounds hit.

Heme took a final pause, waiting.

"Okay, I want you to release the Heavy, hold two secs, then release the Needle at will. On my mark."

Here we go.

Heme took a breath, holding it with lungs that existed only in her mind, a holdover from her days as a regular-duty sniper. She gripped the firing controls with her remaining hand, fingers resting lightly on the trigger.

"Firing."

Heme squeezed.

A slight recoil, and Gun fired. The Heavy round exploded out, horizontal stabilizers springing open. Gun, augmented by the cat brain's reflexes, maneuvered the round with the hyper-reactive twitch adjustments that no human mind could accomplish. Keeping one eye on the target, Heme's mind danced over the HUD's virtual controls, slaving sequential network sensors to track the Heavy's progress.

Three hundred yards out, a microscopic blast of white puffed out of the Heavy's left side, starting its rotation. Heme smiled.

Perfect. Now the Needle

As if hearing her thought, Gun fired the thin projectile, the chrysalis shaking from the recoil. As soon as the round cleared the barrel, the chrysalis released the cable they perched on, and they dropped like a stone, screaming towards the city street below. The chrysalis' wings flared open, catching the wind tunnel's updraft and rocketing them forward, into the flow of traffic. Heme wove them through it, looping underneath the shadow of a transport pod. She followed it as long as she could, throwing out a fabricated taxi ID before peeling off and whispering to a landing on the side of another building.

As the chrysalis made contact with their new perch, Gun pulled the Heavy's optics into Heme's vision, just in time for her to see the projectile slam into the synth-steel, boring a clean hole through it. One hundred and fifty meters behind, the Needle followed the Heavy's path, guided by Gun.

The network immediately responded to the Heavy's assault, as though New Philadelphia were a living thing that had just been shot. Heme watched as Gun threaded the Needle into the hole left by the Heavy, coasting in on the jet stream of a nanobot swarm headed towards the breach. The Needle slipped through, undetected, as the nanobots clotted over the hole.

Their gamble had paid off. The Needle now had a clear shot.

She glanced at readings coming from the target's drone swarm. In the interim, her implant was doing an excellent job with new renderings of the target. Despite the distance, each microdrone within the cloud was tracked and visible, with only a microsecond's delay from real-time.

Movement around their objective caused her to switch focus. The target's cloud was aware of the activity around the injured building, twitching and shifting in response to the Heavy's impact. No sign of countermeasures against the Needle, though.

Good.

"Gun, third stage now. Full power. Get that Needle through that net. I think the swarm realizes something's up."

"Roger. Projectile telemetry is solid. All systems green. I am initiating final stage separation now."

Heme threw her processing capacity behind Gun's, augmenting the weapon as she made final modifications to the Needle's flight computer, all in less than a millisecond.

The Needle's casing pulled away, and its dome opened like a flower. A submicroscopic reaction ignited a chemical engine at the Needle's core. The final stage jetted out, angling for the target at hypersonic speeds. No more flight computer, no more control—just their best final target anticipation and release. The subdermal barb was only two millimeters long and about a thousand angstroms wide, making it impossible to track. Looking through Gun's imaging reticle, Heme saw the glow emanating from the barb—visible only via visual decryption algorithms.

The glow rocketed into the drone swarm. Their calculations were perfect. Heme watched as the barb glided down the projected flight path towards the target's left ear.

The glow vanished, but there was no confirmation of a hit on her screen.

"Gun, what happened? Contact?"

"I think…"

Almost as soon as she asked, data flooded back at her. The swarm reconfigured, spinning in layered stacks of clockwise and counterclockwise movement, save for one small area, a turbulent hub of activity like Jupiter's eye. The area where her Needle had penetrated.

Somehow, they'd intercepted it. But to intercept it, they'd have to track its flight, which was impossible.

How???

"Gun—"

An implosive thud shook the building. The feedback overwhelmed the chrysalis' dampers, shutting it down.

Frantic, Heme did an emergency restart, slicing through the layered protocols and bringing the chrysalis back into full awareness. A dozen critical warnings and errors pounded into her skull. The chrysalis reconnected with the network just as the identical crescents of the building's spires evaporated in the heat of a molten detonation, lighting up the sky—right where the chrysalis had perched on the cable seconds before.

Without thinking, Heme released the chrysalis, allowing it to drop another hundred meters before jetting forward, aiming for an open window on the other side of the flow of traffic. The chrysalis contracted and squeezed as they corkscrewed in. A thud from a near miss shook Heme as they dove into oncoming vessels and aircraft. She silenced the alarms, focused on their flight path.

We're not going to fit!

Mind racing, Heme accessed the building's mainframe and broke into the eightieth floor's northwest wall control module.

Less than a second to impact ... no time for finesse...

The chrysalis, grafted into her own nervous system, responded without hesitation, hacking into the local network and isolating the building around their area of impact. Heme rode in through the chrysalis' data breach, shutting down the wall and creating a sensory anesthesia.

The building felt nothing when they cannonballed through, taking out the window and part of the wall. Their deceleration force would have crushed a human into a paste, but Heme's biomods absorbed the shock as she focused on deploying a chameleon. The small device popped through the chrysalis' skin, replicating and patching the wall before the building's already reawakening systems could trigger a breach alert.

"Okay, Gun. We need a hole. Prep a Bouquet ... The target knows we're here, so we may as well take out the cloud before he finds us."

"Heme, the Needle telemetry is bouncing back. Do you see it? Here, I will pull it up for you."

Gun pushed a crystalline blossom into her central vision: a single data pulse, entangled in background radiation, tattooed with the Needle's ID. Stunned, Heme decrypted the pulse. Data flowed through her implant, saturating her display.

The barb had penetrated the drone cloud after all, and had broadcast once before biodegrading. The target had been resistant to the toxin … another impossibility, unless he knew the attack was coming and had encoded the specific immunoglobulin production into his own cells.

Which meant a leak. One or more of the three people who worked on the toxin. She had to let Franklin command know.

"HEME! BREACH!!!" Gun screamed at her, wiping away her context screen and blowing up the Needle's pulse analysis. Heme recognized the problem right away, but it was too late. Corrupted code was leaking out of the pulse, attacking the chrysalis' neural core.

No … not corrupted … rewritten.

Heme swore, her mind flying in a million directions as she analyzed the pulse.

The target's drones had discovered them. Somehow the target had captured the Needle, cracked the decryption, re-encoded it, and piggybacked the pulse as it ping-ponged through the proxies. No wonder there had been a delay.

Stupid. Rookie move to not quarantine the pulse first.

She pulled up the pulse breakdown. Twenty seconds estimated until their target had a lock on them. Heme ordered the chrysalis to strengthen its connection with the apartment building, and then refocused on the target. There wasn't time.

"Gun, stack an EMP round with the Bouquet. Dial the Bouquet mitosis to a one to one ratio, priority to that drone cloud defense matrix. Set the EMP to broad spectrum. Count of five to release. I want all the survivors down. What's our best shot after this? I need a high-percentile kill option."

"I will try. Difficult to take a shot from this angle. Take a look at ballistics."

Trajectory analysis scrolled across her vision. Heme scanned it, feeling the clock ticking inside her head.

"Not good enough, Gun. Thirty percent fail rate is the least I'll accept. Do it again."

A notice flashed in her retinal HUD: the chrysalis had completed binding with the building. She scanned its work and nodded, satisfied. The building thought the chrysalis was part of the existing structure—for now. With luck, that would buy them a minute.

"Okay, Heme. I have a better firing solution. Take a look." New flight paths blossomed in Heme's eye, spiraling towards the target. It was a complex path, relying on wind patterns more that she liked, but it was less risky.

"Okay. The only thing we have capable of that kind of in-flight maneuverability is our 20 mm round, yes? You have fifteen seconds to modify it with a micronuke. Stack it after the EMP. Pause a quarter second to release. I don't want them to have time to recover."

A small piece of the wall blew inward, sending dust and debris into the room. Heme froze Gun in place and shoved the chrysalis's non-essentials into hibernation.

The drone cloud had found them.

For a few moments, nothing appeared to happen, and then a small black clot, the size of a pinhead, oozed through. It paused, hovering in front of the hole. It shuddered and grew, shifting into a complex, multifaceted geode the size of a small fist.

The drone wafted forward, settling on a chair. It extended a silver-black proboscis and sampled a piece of the table before moving forward again. It repeated the procedure, sampling the floor, then a piece of the wall, making its way over to the chrysalis.

Aware of the time draining away until the target backtracked to them through the corrupted pulse, Heme continued to hold, watching and waiting.

The drone floated over to them, as though gliding on a summer breeze. It hesitated and descended, proboscis first, onto the chrysalis' skin. The proboscis bored in, and the drone took a sample.

Now.

Heme's lips formed the word as she shot the order to the chrysalis. The drone jumped as it sensed the chrysalis move, but it was too late. The chrysalis engulfed it like an ameba, consuming it.

Immediately, the chrysalis began to assimilate and replicate the drone's signal. Heme willed herself to wait, watching precious microseconds bleed out as the chrysalis struggled to get a lock on the drone, which thrashed around inside a containment cell. After a moment, the drone's "OK" signal pulsed out ... a perfect mimic. It was almost seamless in real-time, but eons had passed inside Heme's head. With the signal replicated, Heme's entire body relaxed.

"Gun, get a lock. Light the rounds."

"Rounds are hot. I have the 20 mm round augmented with a micronuke warhead. EMP bomb is loaded ahead of it. Targeting the electronics of the drone cloud."

In the corner of her vision, Heme saw the confirmation of each round's active status tick. She glanced at her clock. Thirty seconds until the pulse had them painted and ID'd, dead to rights.

Just enough time for me to flash interrogate the drone.

"Gun, we fire in fifteen, right before the target reaches that building. Final flight check. As soon as you release the micronuke, I want you to load our last Heavy; set it for five-yard burst, antegrade thermal pattern."

"You sure about that, Heme? The safety mechanism will not let the round fire that close to us."

"Override the safety block. I know, we'll be in the blast zone. That's the idea. We're going to fake our own death."

Heme turned to the drone. She queued up a series of commands and the chrysalis extended itself into the building's network, completely overwhelming what re-mained of the apartment building's security and inserting itself into the superstructure's computing core.

Heme allowed herself a microsecond of self-satis-faction.

One of the benefits of military hardware … the brute force option.

She slaved the building's computing capacity to the chrysalis and bored into the drone. Another second dropped off the clock, but the intensity of her focus made it an abstract concept.

The drone lay before her, a tangled mass of data and networked connections. Focusing through the lens of the building's computing power, she cut into the drone, separating its protocols from its defense matrices.

And then … there it was. The answer to the drone's perfect camouflage: their total adaptability.

The computational power of the entire local area was integrated into the drone network, from the largest skyscrapers down to an individual's personal augments. Every last iota of data was manipulated through the drone swarm, using whatever computational ability lay within a block's radius of the target.

Unbelievable.

And then the solution hit her.

"Gun … the drones don't have any sensors them-selves. They're tapping into New Philadelphia! They're slaving every sensor and building around them to do the processing! *That's* how they can pull off that level of cam-ouflage!"

"So. How do we get around that? With that kind of ability, the target will see us coming as soon as we fire."

"Okay, here's what I want you to do: reverse the order. Fire the EMP first, but I want a double shot. We have three of them, right? Load two, each set at a forty-five-de-gree complementary dispersion field—ninety degrees total pulse spread. I want to hit as much around the target as possible. I don't care about the drones. Follow it with the Bouquet, immediately. Pause three seconds, release the 20 mm micronuke, fastest trajectory to get it on the target. I don't care what you have to bounce off. Skip preflight. Light the rounds. Give me a green when ready."

"Got it. Hang on. Loading the second EMP. I am re-programming their dispersal pattern."

Another thump shook her chest as the rounds woke up. The icons lit up again on her heads up display, ticking green one by one as Gun chambered them in her barrel.

Good girl. Way to adapt to my impulsive changes. Not bad for a young AI.

"Rounds are hot. Fire when ready."

Heme sighted through the optics. Took in a mental breath. Held it.

"Firing."

She squeezed the trigger.

The first EMP rocketed out, with the second pressed against it. Heme watched as the two rounds separated, flying parallel to each other as they wove through the midday traffic.

The noses split, spreading wide, engines flaring as wind resistance increased.

Heme held her breath, watching Gun twist and curve the projectiles around buildings and obstacles, trying to bring the EMP arrays to bear.

Her HUD flashed red.

The target had found her. Heme ignored it, focusing on ballistics.

"Firing."

The familiar tremor of recoil raced through her body as Gun launched the Bouquet.

The EMPs streaked head on towards the target. The drone cloud began to respond, forming a wall in front of the target.

Too late, suckers...

"Activating the EMP."

Gun triggered the projectiles, and the devices exploded. A shockwave sizzled out in a wide cone pattern, knocking out every electrical device in its path. Three full city blocks died. Lights went black, screens went dark, and vehicles dropped out of the air mid-flight, like a shower of man-made meteors. Heme tried not to think about who was inside as they went crashing into the ground below—hundreds of balls of fire, lighting up the darkened lower city.

Shaking it off, Heme refocused on the targeting reticle. There was no time to mourn strangers. She saw the drone cloud shifting, morphing as it pivoted to face her location. Somehow, they had resisted the EMP.

"Firing the micronuke."

Another tremor as the projectile shot out of Gun's barrel.

The datastream told her the cloud was about to shoot at her. Time was up. The drones fired. Billions of tiny particles shot out, fusing into a molten mass that plowed through everything in front of it. Heme winced as it crashed through a residential building, bursting out the other side, right towards them.

Heme braced herself for the hit, and then frowned as the chrysalis projected the impact point.

A fraction of a second later, the mass exploded three hundred yards away from her. A two-hundred-and-forty-story office structure folded in two as the mass struck it halfway down.

They really are blind. They're guessing based on where the EMP came from.

The drone cloud adjusted its aim. Gun ran impact calculations, projecting the results on Heme's HUD. She was right in the center of the projected impact.

"I see it, Gun. Hold position. Wait for our rounds to hit..."

Just then, the Bouquet split apart, each piece undergoing mitosis and mushrooming into a glistening sheet of particles streaking towards the target.

Impact.

Millions of tiny slivers of shrapnel impaled the drone cloud. Countless microscopic explosions burst around the target as the drones' fission drives overloaded. Standing at the center, as ash fell around him, a thin, small man squinted out to where Heme was hidden somewhere in the jungle of the cityscape.

She saw him moving his hands, twisting and manipulating, the movements telegraphing his panic.

I bet it's been a very long time since he's been afraid.

"He's doing something to the whole block, Heme."

Klaxons sounded in the apartment building, and the walls around her turned red. The room peeled away, and a storm cloud of drones of all kinds coalesced around them from every direction, like angry bees.

She turned her gaze back to the reticle, just as the micronuke impacted. A look of shock crossed the man's face as a hole blossomed in his chest.

The micronuke exploded, and the man vaporized.

The chrysalis convulsed again as Gun fired the Heavy straight into the oncoming drone cloud. In slow motion, Heme watched as it left Gun's barrel, spiraling out and spraying propellant. A flash, and the propellant ignited. The round exploded, the radius of the blast ejecting forward, as Heme had programmed it to do. Still, some of the blast came backward, blowing a hole through the wall and slamming into the chrysalis. Heme was ready.

She engaged the chrysalis, and it leaped forward out of the hole even as the wall was still disintegrating, driving the chrysalis into free-fall. She engaged its thrusters and pulled a hard one-eighty, firing straight back up through the Heavy's expanding debris cloud.

Heedless of the gravitational strain on the chrysalis, she pushed the throttle wide open, rocketing through the debris cloud and out beyond, arcing straight up into the gray sky. Drones of various sizes and shapes attempted to give chase, firing at her as she blasted past. They punched through the heavy cloud cover, smashing through a rain-seeding array, and then they were free, climbing upward beyond the reach of the drones.

Stratosphere, mesosphere, thermosphere, exosphere, vacuum.

And just like that, it's over.

Heme cut back on the throttle as the chrysalis settled into stable orbit. She issued a few commands, and the chrysalis reconfigured, blending into the endless sea of space debris that circled Earth.

"Gun, send a tightbeam to command. Tell them know we're Butcher Block Red; target is down."

Pickup wouldn't be for another week, after everything settled down. Plenty of time to finally relax after months of tension. Systems powered down as her own mind began to cycle into hibernation mode. Remaining at full power meant a chance of discovery, and discovery wasn't worth it—no matter how minute the chance.

Gun nudged her mind, purring. Heme chuckled to herself.

Gotta learn to control that cat brain, Gun.

Heme stroked her weapon, running mental fingers across her back. Her consciousness faded as hibernation triggered.

"Good job, Gun. That's my girl."

ACT 2

....

LOSS

*O*nce, all I had to do for food was order it to my house.

Sam sighted down his scope, aiming his airgun at a post-human thrashing around four stories below. Occasional flashes of the massive creature appeared under a swarm of ants, blood flowing from a hundred bites. The ground and ants were slick with it. He clicked forward once on the scope's focus knob and the picture sharpened just in time to see one of the thing's five heads—a middle-aged woman with graying hair—ripped off by one of the bull ants clinging to it.

Lifting his eyes from the scope, Sam craned his neck left and right down Leopold Street. An endless stream of ants crawled everywhere on the road, heading north.

A chorus of warbling, almost-human cries drew him back. The post-human, despite a presumed intelligence given its five—now four—heads, was trying to eat the offending ant, its cavernous chest sucking wetly as it pulled in the ant.

That's not a good idea, dude.

A fresh wave of ants smothered the melee. The post-human surged up, ripping ants apart at random with its twenty arms. The hole in its chest had resealed, having managed to consume the meal. More ants swarmed, the bulls forming a protective circle while harvesters streamed around them.

The post-human did its weird warble-chorus again, and its shoulder exploded in a haze of blood and tissue. Inside the bleeding crater, the consumed bull ant whipped around, tearing at her captor. Sam almost whistled in admiration, before catching himself. No unnecessary noise. Not now, when he was this close.

The fight moved up the street, carried by the flow of the river of ants, still providing him with an opportunity to make a shot. Sam reshouldered his air rifle, looking for a target.

There would be plenty of bull ants on the street, which would be fine for the hemolymph, but this was a rare opportunity, a distraction that might net him a special kill. Sam panned a little way down from the fight, where countless broken bull ants marked the post-human's destructive path. The stream of ants was a little more chaotic here, disorganized by the intense reek of the dead and dying's pheromones.

There. A nursing ant, its pincers holding foamy green sponge in a tight grip. Sam glanced through his rangefinder, trying to keep the ant in view. Sixty-eight yards. Doable. The air rifle, a high-pressure .45 bullpup, was designed for people with a fetish for nostalgic, retro big game hunting.

Countless years ago, when he'd bought the gun, he'd reasoned he'd be too much of a chicken to kill himself with it. His friends had thought it was some statement on individuality. Sam had let them think that, since talking about killing oneself in the pre-apocalypse time meant forced hospitalization and neural remapping.

None of that mattered now. His friends were long dead, part of some post-human, and yet here he was, sighting through the rifle he'd thought was too weak to kill him.

Sam took in a breath, letting the old bitterness fade. He held it, counted to three, and pulled the trigger. The gun's bolt clanked as the bolt cycled. There was no big boom; it was always the anticlimax of the hunt. A heartbeat passed before the nursing ant staggered. A hit. Sam exhaled, watching the ant weave against its hive-mates. Four yards later, it went down. Sam panned around, seeing if the shot had attracted attention. Bull ants were one thing, but a nursing ant's death tended to whip the colony into a frenzy.

Sure enough, a boil of agitation started around the stricken insect. Sam brought his gun down and pulled himself closer to the shooter's slit in the hunter's blind, watching with a concerned eye.

More warbling. The post-human was in three pieces now, each one fighting with a ferocity only seen in those facing death. A few yards away, by the nursing ant, the agitation swept through the sea of ants like a living thing. Sam's heart beat faster despite himself as the post-human edged towards him, the pheromone-induced maelstrom sucking in all the insects in its path.

Come on … go for the obvious threat.

For a moment it looked like the ants were onto him, then the post-human warbled again, drawing the attention of the seething ball of ants.

There you go.

Seconds later, a pink mist was all that remained of the monster. A minute later, even that was gone, leaving only the unending stream of ants.

Satisfied he had not attracted unwanted attention, Sam stood, staying low under the wall of the hunter's blind. He slung his rifle over his shoulder and moved inside, easing the heavy door closed behind him.

A cascade of refracted light greeted him as he entered his sanctuary. Thousands of prisms hung in windows that offered a circumferential view of the crumbling city. The prisms, painstakingly collected over the years, captured the molding light of the mutating atmosphere and filtered it into a fractaled rainbow. Light spread everywhere across the enormous room he'd dubbed "The Alamo." Deep down, Sam knew those prisms kept the world out, filtering clean the rot trying to get in and break him.

The Alamo was the fourth floor of a downtown New Philadelphia office building, converted with laborious care and years of labor. He'd cleared out all the extra walls, creating a few thousand feet of open space he'd sectioned off into different areas: armory and workshop, kitchen, bedroom, and—his pride and joy—the library, which took up almost a quarter of the space. Books had been considered obsolete in pre-apocalypse civilization, but he'd found a cache of them and, despite the risks, had hauled them all back.

"Hello, Samuel. How was it?"

"Hi, Tes. Got a nurse while a post-human was doing its wrecking ball thing. A ton of bull ants died too … we should plan on at least ten hours to harvest everything."

"I observed the end of it on the northeast monitor; quite a fight."

"Sure was. I'm going to recharge the rifle and get some things done. Everything calm?"

"Yes. No sensors tripped."

Years ago, Sam had found an undisturbed Tesla-manufactured mercenary's chrysalis during a week-long expedition into an area of New Philadelphia about sixty miles away. It had been an incredible find. He'd spent days trying to get it flying again but, like most other singularity-era machines, it was too complex for a human to fix.

However, during his fumbling attempt, he'd discovered that the chrysalis's main weapon AI, housed in a cat's brain, was still alive and clinging to the edges of sanity after years of sensory isolation. He'd rescued it, named it Tes, and nursed her back to health. It had been common practice for biotech companies to assign pre-apocalypse AIs a gender. It had taken a few weeks after recovery before

Tes had remembered hers. In return for his help, she'd saved him from the oceans of loneliness and depression he'd been fighting for years.

Now Tes inhabited an eight-legged bomb disposal droid with a fusion battery—another unlikely find. She skittered behind Sam as he walked over to a workbench piled high with neat stacks of scrap lead.

"Running low on rifle rounds, Tes. Used four today … missed three times. I know, I know, I don't need to hear it. There's still plenty of lead in the armory. We're going to have to smelt some more rounds, though, before the week's out."

He handed Tes the weapon, and she extended a plug, locking into the weapon's air tank. A slight hiss suffused the air as she filled it.

"I will perform weapons maintenance as well, Samuel."

"Okay, thanks. I'm gonna check the bag, then."

Sam opened a closet and grabbed an old, green external-frame backpack. One by one, he pulled everything out, inspecting each item. It was a soothing ritual, as close as he could get to meditation. Each item was hard won from years of scavenging: a compressed air tank for refills, extra lead pellets, a pitted and rusted grenade he'd bartered for years ago, a knife, and a Nalgene bottle filled with filtered hemolymph. Survival gear. Equipment for food harvesting. A compact consciousness module he'd modified to carry Tes's consciousness.

"Hey, girl. When you're done there, fill up the high-pressure tank. It's at four thousand right now. Might be a slow leak … can you check on that, too?"

"I will if you stop calling me 'girl.' I'm an adult AI … not to mention older than you, as you've obviously forgotten. Also, I control the ethylene oxide, remember?"

Sam chuckled as he repacked the backpack. He couldn't help pushing her buttons sometimes. Tes gave as good as she got, though. She was a bit of a practical joker, something that always took him by surprise.

"Okay, okay. Yes, ma'am. I'm taking a nap before tonight. What's the activity been like the last week? The ogres staying quiet? Pretty weird to see one of them during the day today."

"Normal patterns across sensory areas three through four. Slight traffic in area nine. Seismograph estimates a creature with a mass in the six-hundred-kilogram range. Peak activity at twenty-three hundred hours to zero three hundred."

"That's good. What about the immediate four-block grid? Areas one, two, and five?"

"Negative detection for eight days between twenty-two hundred hours and dawn."

"Perfect. Nine o'clock, then. Wake me. We'll be on the roof by ten."

Sam always got the jitters before leaving the safety of the Alamo. There was no good time to do it—even more so now that the world had been degrading for two decades. The post-humans seemed to prefer the night, but, according to sensors he'd placed in a five-mile radius around his holdout, they were few and far between. It was better odds than the ants.

About five years ago, he'd come to an intersection and found a woman pulling the inner tube off a bicycle tire. Sam had seen her from a block away—he'd been trying to haul a solar array back to the Alamo. She'd been the first human he'd seen in at least a year. The excitement of seeing another living human being had overwhelmed him, and he'd run to her, waving a white scarf over his head like a maniac to tell her he wasn't a threat. She saw him, looked up, and had smiled before turning her head towards something out of his view, a frown on her face. A second later, a swarm of ants had engulfed her, flooding the road and walls before disappearing down the street.

The entire thing had only taken seconds, but Sam had stayed in the middle of the road, paralyzed by fear, for another half hour. Eventually, he'd regained control of himself and fled, leaving his wheelbarrow and solar array. It was still there, sitting where it had been abandoned, a decaying memorial to the woman's last moments.

After that, Sam had stopped going out during the day. Despite the risks. Despite the absolute horror that walked around in the dark. He couldn't do it anymore.

"Go sleep, Samuel. I will wake you." Tes always seemed to sense his moods.

"Fine," Sam said grudgingly.

He kicked off his shoes and walked over to his bedroom: a permasteel shipping container he'd cut apart, dragged up to the fourth floor, and then re-welded together. Ducking low, he went through the narrow door, sliding it closed behind him and locking it.

"Lock the door, Samuel."

"You realize you say that every single night, right? I've been doing this for years … you don't need to remind me. Variety is the spice of life, Tes!"

"Lock the door, Samuel."

"Holy cow, you're impossible. Done."

His bedroom doubled as a panic room: a last-ditch holdout if the ants, post-humans, or whatever other hellish abomination broke through. It was a useless gesture—Sam had seen post-humans punch through walls like tissue paper, but it made him feel better. Every other avenue and door in the building was also welded shut, and Sam had spent months filling in the other floors with debris and seeding them with directional hydrogen mines he'd found.

You're a paranoid coward.
Yeah, but cowards survive.
Sleep came quickly.

The New Philadelphia national anthem startled him awake during its ugly, discordant crescendo, as it always did. One of Tes's weird personality quirks was her steadfast patriotism to the former super-city, no doubt because she'd been a member of its armed forces. Or, at least, he thought it was a personality quirk. Deep down, he suspected she got a kick out of waking him up like that. Sam groaned, pulling his pillow over his head.

"I'm up, Tes. You know what would be awesome? Never hearing that grotesque noise again."

"It is twenty-one-hundred hours, Samuel. Sensors are clear, save for the expected activity in section nine."

"Did you hear what I said? You should really play someth—Ah, never mind."

Fumbling around and reminding himself for the millionth time to bring a flashlight into the pitch black room, he changed shirts for a synthskin tactical vest with heavy lumps sewn into the spine. After adjusting the straps, Sam undid the lock and emerged from the panic room, stretching. "You ready?"

"I rechecked your gear. Also repaired a microfracture in the high-pressure tank around the inlet valve."

"Great, thanks. Go ahead and move into the flight computer. I've had it charging since last week, so no worries about running out of juice if we have to book it."

Rule number one when scavenging: always be prepared to never return home.

"Hey, did the vest charge after that battery replacement?" Sam asked.

"Yes. Transferring."

Sam grabbed the external-frame backpack, securing the straps. He jumped up and down, testing the straps, and then walked over to the main door. The former elevator door to the building was now also a massive chunk of permasteel. He took a helmet with six bulbous lenses mounted on it off a hook next to the door and seated it on his head, dropping the lenses over his eyes. The well-worn webbing scratched his head and stank of sour sweat. Feeling on the side of the helmet, he twisted a cracked dial until it clicked. Sam fished around behind the helmet until he found two wires, twisted them together, and tucked the filaments into the goggles' webbing. A small reticle lit up on a screen in front of his eyes, flickering and stabilizing into an image of the room, overlaid with data from his sensor network. He turned to a mirror on the wall, inspecting himself to make sure everything was there. The reflectionless black optics of the night vision goggles stared back at him.

Bony guy in a much patched gray-orange jumpsuit, check. Patchy beard with a chunk missing where he'd burned himself, check. Gun, check. Gear, check. Boots...

Oh yeah. Shoes. How the heck have I survived so long?

He grabbed a pair of well-worn boots covered in tape and put them on.

"Tes, can you hear me? Night goggles are up. I'm ready if you are."

"I am in the computer. We will see if your new transmitter will keep us linked to the Alamo while we are away. I have a pretty good connection right now."

"That's right! I can't believe I forgot about it! Okay, let's go."

Sam paused, cleared his throat, and bowed his head. He always felt awkward doing this. "Hey, God. Guide us while we're out there. Protect us. Bring us back. Also ... please let us meet another living human. Please."

"Amen. Opening the door, Samuel."

"Thanks, girl."

"Samuel. That is insulting. Also, I have no skin for you to get under. I don't know why you try."

"Haha, I'll stop calling you 'girl' if you call me 'Sam.' Samuel makes me feel like one of those anti-technology people. Remember those guys and the sandwich signs they'd wear?"

"I cannot help it, Samuel. You remind me of one of those anti-technology people. Remember how obsessed they were with prisms and crystals?"

Sam laughed out loud as the huge door retracted into the wall without a sound. When he'd built the door, it had taken weeks of troubleshooting to get rid of the squeaks. It had never broken down or made the slightest sound when moved, and each time he opened it he still got a small wave of self-satisfaction.

He turned on his flashlight and stepped into a narrow metal room. Tes closed the reinforced door behind him. Sam shone the light up, revealing the dull sheen of sheet metal rising in a four-foot-wide shaft into the darkness. Eight-inch metal pegs poked out at regular intervals all the way up. This was another creation of his—the only entrance and exit. Sam had converted the elevator shaft, narrowing it using debris from nearby buildings. He'd lined the shaft with sheet metal after noticing that ants couldn't climb the slick surface.

Post-humans were a different matter, but he was ready for them in other ways. Sam popped open a small panel next to the door, pulling down on a lever. The small click confirmed the door was now booby-trapped. If tripped, ethylene oxide scavenged from a sterilizer would explode, releasing an ultra-toxic vapor that would kill anything inside the shaft. Sam replaced the panel and climbed up, counting the ladder rungs. At twelve, he stopped and with ginger care unscrewed the rung, disarming the detonator inside. After replacing it, he kept moving, pausing twice more to disable one trap and set another.

After fifteen laborious minutes—two stories—Sam reached the inch-thick door sealing the shaft from the outside.

"Okay, Tes. Still got data coming from the Alamo?"

"I do, Samuel. You are clear."

"I'm just going to double check … no offense."

Sam opened another panel and turned on the monitor inside. A series of images popped on-screen—infrared, heat, motion, showing all areas of the roof and walls.

No blind spots. He'd spent hours calculating video angles. Everything was dead still.

"Okay, Tes. Open it up."

The heavy metal door rose with a quiet whirr.

The night sky came into view, a congealed starlessness broken only by the oily green of the moon. After watching Earth's atmosphere mutate for almost two decades, Sam was beginning to suspect it was the result of terraforming complexes run amok ... complexes like the ones that had terraformed the moon. Sam could still remember the awe he'd felt as a kid, looking through his telescope, watching the enormous machines move across the pale white-gray orb, leaving paths of brown and green in their wake.

I wonder what happened to the colonists up there.

Not that it mattered now. Sam clicked off his flashlight and climbed out, crouching low. He tuned his goggles, tightening the on-screen image until it was clear. After taking a second to run through his mental checklist, he scanned the rooftops and horizon in all directions. Nothing.

A decade ago, the last time he'd talked to another living human, he'd briefly shared a shelter with a man who loved to tell wild stories about post-humans who could jump from building to building, and others who could even fly. About some post-humans without stomachs, who would just vomit acid on their victims, then absorb the resulting mushy mess through their skin. About how they could graft to each other, sometimes getting as big as buildings. At the time, Sam had blown him off as a fabulist. Here on the roof, years later, surrounded by dark, Sam could see the things from the stories in his mind's eye, just behind him ... just out of sight. It was worse because he now knew they were real.

The guy had also told Sam there was a safe haven in South America. Some of the survivors had managed to build machines that surrounded the whole continent, keeping the terraforming rot at bay.

There'd been a million safe haven rumors, though. All false. Sam could remember being doubtful at the time ... still a skeptic even after all he'd been through. Years change a person, though. He was a believer now, as far as the nightmares in the city went. The Alamo's fortifications could attest to that. Two weeks after the talk about the South American refuge, Sam saw the guy again—he couldn't remember his name—melding into the leg of a post-human. Actually, he didn't recognize *him*, just his tattoo: an amazing full-color back piece of a roaring tiger. Sam never went looking for the South American safe haven. He had a dozen reasons why, but deep down he knew it was just a cover for his cowardice.

Shoving the memories back, Sam picked his way through neat stacks of boxes. He passed between dry pots of earth, his latest failed attempt to grow food, and stepped over the melted remains of a prison where he'd once held a post-human the size of a large dog. Everything on the roof was low to the ground, packed tightly together. He'd left no room for anything to hide, giving him a clear panoramic view of the city ruins from any position.

He took his time, but still quickly reached the north-facing retaining wall and pulled his goggles up from his eyes. The quality of the goggles' image dropped off dramatically at fifty yards, pretty much useless for anything other than close quarters. Sam's eyes adjusted, and he waited. Smelled. Listened. Post-humans had a distinct odor, which was usually the first sign they were nearby. He stayed there for five minutes, soaking up the moon's murky green light and concentrating on sensing everything around him.

The crumbled buildings remained stoically immobile. Not a hint of life, not a twitch of movement. Just the flat, strange stale smell of the new atmosphere. Time to go down.

Sam pulled the goggles back down and removed the canvas cover from the elevator controls. After measuring the battery charge, he went through the checklist. A checklist for everything—another survival skill. Backup systems, emergency return, pulley grease, primary drive system. All checked out. He opened the small door and climbed in. After another quick scan, Sam flipped the lever, and the elevator eased down the side of the building, powered by the ultra-quiet Tesla drive engine that had flown Tes's chrysalis.

Nearing the ground, the elevator slowed to a halt with a soft bump on a rubber mat. Sam exited with the air-gun drawn, his right eye goggle's optics slaved to the air rifle's scope.

"Find me that nursing ant, Tes."

After a moment's pause, a red dot marking the nursing ant's location lit up on his screen.

"Sensors are quiet, Samuel. I've still got great signal strength from the Alamo."

Sam moved down the street, staying off the main road and away from the crumpled forms of fallen bull ants. Experience had taught him never to assume anything was dead—even when it was in pieces. The nursing ant was by itself, lying propped up against a wall. Sam crouched six yards away, gun aimed at its head, and mentally counted to twenty while watching for movement.

"Anything?"

"No signs of life. Also, looks like everything we've passed is dead," Tes said.

Sam approached the ant with caution, taking his time, until he was close enough to touch it. He poked it with the rifle's barrel. No response. Sam unslung his backpack and propped it against the ant's body.

"Big one, Tes. Gotta be at least five feet long."

The ant's pincers contained the prize—the masticated food the ants made and fed to their larvae. High in protein and carbs, rich in fat.

"At least thirty pounds of food here."

Sam reached into his backpack and grabbed an elastic bag. Stretching it open, he stuffed it until it brimmed with the dense green sponge. The sack closed with difficulty; the seals were old and worn. Sam crouched down and set up a small pump and hose next to the carcass. He connected it to the sponge-filled sack and turned the pump on, aspirating all the air and condensing it down to the size of a brick. He capped it and put it in his backpack, reaching for another empty set.

"If possible I'd like to make three or four trips, Tes. There's enough hemolymph here to keep us off the streets for months."

He took a long, hollow auger and shoved it through the ant's thorax, attaching it to the pump. The pump whined low as it sucked the liquid contents out of the ant, filling the containers until they looked like five watermelon-sized grapes, stretched taught. He paused, studying them with a practiced eye.

"I'll just get the raw stuff now. We'll process it back home. This is all about getting as much as possible."

Sam exchanged the full bags for empty ones, shifted the auger to a new site, and restarted the pump. While those were filling, he grabbed a net and a flat panel with a glistening bottom out of the backpack. He unfolded the panel into a large square and laid it on the ground. After placing ten hemolymph bags in the net bag, he set them on the square.

"Okay, Tes. Take it back. I'm going for that bull up the street."

"Sensors are clear. I'll deposit these on the roof for now."

The square lifted, the air underneath it blurring. It took off without a sound, weaving among the dead ants, angling towards the elevator. A sub-screen on Sam's display opened, tracking the hemolymph's progress.

Sam approached the next ant, and the same ritual repeated, the AI and human working with little further communication as the globes of hemolymph piled up on the roof.

After three hours, Sam had worked up to where the post-human had met its end. He could see residuals of the thing scattered around him, but none were big enough to pose a threat. In his experience, post-human flesh needed to be about the size of his fist to have enough life to begin to re-assimilate. The ants appeared to have somehow known this, as they had vaporized it through the sheer savagery of their attack.

The bull ant he was currently working on was missing half her abdomen, but it still had a great deal of fluid. It was just taking a little more work to get it all out; Sam had already repositioned the auger twice and was about to do it a third time when section two pinged.

Tes was immediately in his ear.

"Samuel, large presence, over the thousand-kilogram minimum, seventy yards as the crow flies at nine o'clock, two-forty yards from your position if it takes the main road."

Almost simultaneous with her voice, a rolling tide of flesh-rot hit him, making him retch.

"Seems closer than that. How'd it penetrate this far without the sensors picking it up? I'm getting my mask out and moving to the elevator."

He reached into his pack, pulling out a respirator and strapping it on below the goggles. Sam pressed a button under his chin, felt it suction lightly to his face, and cool air started circulating.

"Okay, I'm—"

"Cease verbal, Samuel. Dorsal heat patterns changed. It is accelerating. It is on you. Text only. You cannot make it to the elevator. Find an alternative, now." Fear and concern saturated Tes's voice, and his heart jumped into his throat. She didn't get worried easily.

Sam keyed in a command, switching to text response. He flexed his gloved hand, testing the controls while jogging towards the office building, not caring about stealth anymore. Using the ant bodies as cover, he zig-zagged down the street, trying to keep from imagining a wounded ant biting his arm off. If it came to it, being killed by an ant would be a mercy compared to the alternative.

<On text. I can make the elevator. Moving.>

"I would not advise that, Samuel. It is forty seconds from rounding the corner. You are ninety-five yards... What are you doing?"

Sam paused in front of an enormous bull ant and pulled out his knife. Without stopping to think about it, he slashed his forearm, letting the blood drip all over the insect.

<Going for elevator. Clear the bags off.>

"You'll compromise the Alamo, Samuel."

Sam grabbed a clotting bandage, wrapping it around the cut. He pulled the synthskin sleeve down over the bulk. The shirt responded, compressing down hard on the cut to staunch the bleeding.

<Dead out here. Set elevator height three feet. Pull it hard when I'm on.>

Sam ran.

"Hide in a bull ant, Samuel."

<It can smell me. You know that. Almost there.>

Ahead of him, gleaming in the goggles' artificial brightness, the elevator waited three feet off the ground. Beyond it, at the corner of the office building, a fleshy protrusion emerged onto the street.

He jumped, the gel pad at the base of the elevator softening his landing.

Tes immediately began hauling him up. Sam watched as his altitude ticked, afraid to see what was coming.

At the fourth floor, right as he was passing his prism-filled windows, the thing stepped into view, yards away from him.

<Full stop.>

Butcher Block Green

Tes froze the controls, leaving him suspended against the side of the building, swaying gently.

The post-human was enormous. Hundreds of bodies, maybe thousands had grafted themselves into it. Innumerable legs, spread haphazardly under its enormous abdomen, allowed it to move with a surprising grace as it turned the corner onto the main road. The thing had no head of its own—just a solid mass of heads fused together. Impossible arms, altogether too long and thin, reached out and gripped buildings on either side of the street, pulling it along. For such a large creature, its speed was obscene.

Sam twitched, fighting to calm the terror threatening to take over his body. Deep, primal fear. Uncontrollable. It took everything in him to remain quiet and still.

Nothing to do now. It was out of his hands.

God, protect me. Let it pass by me. Please.

Sam opened his eyes. He hadn't realized he'd closed them. He looked up.

An enormous mottled mass of flesh, bone, eyes, hair, and teeth regarded him from a yard away. Sam became aware of the sound of hundreds of distorted windpipes struggling to breathe. Time froze. The smell of the post-human seeped in, despite the respirator's air-tight seal. Sam fought the urge to vomit.

"It's probing ahead, Sam. It's not looking at you. Stay still."

That's the first time she's ever called me Sam...

A fused head, one staring right at him, screamed. The sound built as the scream continued, building and building in volume until the head's bulging eyes bled. Still, it screamed in a violent crescendo as its gaze bored into Sam.

I'm done. It sees me.

And then, like it never existed, the post-human disappeared. Sam blinked.

<PULLMEUPPULLMEUP!!!!!!>

"No, Samuel. No can do. It found your blood. I think your diversion is working. We have to wait."

Feeling foolish in the midst of his abject terror, Sam remembered he had telemetry, and switched his goggles' view to the cameras on the office roof. He flipped through the images, until he could see the post-human, which looked for all the world like an enormous grub with a fur of human legs and thin spider arms, poking at the blood-spattered bull ant below. At the corner of the image, Sam could see himself, huddled in the elevator.

"I do not know how it did not see you, either, Samuel."

How does she do that??

"It's leaving."

Sure enough, the huge creature flowed down the street, appearing satisfied with Sam's diversion.

Sam let out a huge breath he didn't know he'd been holding, and for a moment his vision went blurry.

<I can't believe I just survived that.>

"We. I am in your backpack, remember?"

<Yeah, I don't know what I'd do without you, Tes. I owe you.>

"I know. I need a bigger jar to hold all the favors you owe me."

<Did you just make a joke? Now? Really?>

In the distance, the creature disappeared into the thick darkness.

"It is in section six, moving quite fast. I am unsure how it made it this close without picking up on the sensors. It was right on top of us. It is possible it has been there for weeks, incubating. I am reviewing old data," Tes said.

Sam toggled the text control, switching the mic back on.

"You do that. I'm leaving the hemolymph on the roof for now. It'll be safe until tomorrow night. I need to crash. That was too much."

The elevator clicked into its retaining clamps at the top of the office. Sam stepped out on shaky legs, the relief and tension from back on friendly ground almost overwhelming him.

"Roof clear?" His voice was paper dry.

"According to sensors and imagery, yes."

Sam climbed back into the elevator shaft and triggered the door. The heavy permasteel eased down, sighing as it pressed into the rubber gasket, sealing them in. Sam worked his way down the shaft, checking entry triggers, disabling traps, re-enabling others. Coming down was a more difficult process than climbing up and, for the thousandth time, Sam mentally promised himself he would rebuild it.

Finally, he reached the bottom, muscles shaking from the effort and the post-terror adrenaline crash.

"Open the door, Tes."

"Disable the ethylene oxide first, Samuel."

"Oh, wow … completely forgot. Okay, done."

The door hissed open, and a kaleidoscope of refracted light entered the shaft, illuminating it and immediately lifting Sam's spirits.

Home.

"Do you think we should attempt another trip tomorrow?" Tes asked.

Sam walked in and dropped the backpack to the ground, slumping into a chair as the shaft door closed. He pushed up the goggles, letting them slide until they fell onto the back of the chair.

"No way. We're done. At least until we figure out how something that massive got so deep inside our sensor network. We've got three months of hemolymph there, if we cure it well."

"Samuel…"

"You back in your body yet? Grab me some lymph to drink. My legs are killing me … I need more exercise."

"SAM! The library!"

Tesla chrysalis weapons systems had cutting-edge AI, with built-in emotional inflections designed to better communicate, even though most of them were nonverbal. Sam had never heard that tone in Tes's voice before. He bolted up, whipping around in his chair towards the shelves of books.

In between the first rows, a huge bull ant stood watching them, her knotted, scarred exoskeleton a black hole that swallowed the refracted light playing across it.

"How...?" The question froze on Sam's lips. His eyes shifted left, to where his gun lay twenty feet away, and then right, to his panic room, fifty feet away. The ant would be on top of him before he'd make it three steps.

Survival 101: NEVER *have your gun out of immediate reach. Come on, Sam.*

It remained motionless, its multifaceted eyes fixed on them. Time stood still as they regarded each other like gunfighters in a duel. To his left, Tes began to stand up, positioning herself to make a run for his rifle. She was close, only a couple feet, but it still wasn't close enough...

Tes, no...

She moved with superhuman speed, as her military-grade body was designed to do. Drive legs moving in a blur, she flew past the gun. Tes scooped it up as she went by, creating distance between her and the insect even as she twisted her body around, cocking the gun and bringing it to bear.

The ant was faster, on top of her before Sam had reached down to grasp the combat knife in his boot. Sam heard a sharp crack and a hiss of expanding gas as the gun was bitten in half. The ant tossed its head, ripping the broken gun out of Tes's manipulator arms. It crashed on the wall with violent force, but Sam's eyes were glued to where the creature stood with one armored claw pressing Tes flat, right over her neural core.

Tes, transfer to the consciousness module. Come on, girl.

The AI twitched under the ant's pressure, and the armored leg pressed harder onto the robotic body. The insect's head remained fixed on Sam, its alien eyes unreadable.

Under the ant, Tes went limp.

Good girl.

He wracked his brain, trying to come up with a plan for something he'd never anticipated. Silence permeated the room—no alarms had been triggered ... how on Earth had the ant made it in? The plan for a breach, such as it was, involved releasing the ethylene oxide after he was safely sealed in the bedroom/panic room. No chance of it now.

The ant stayed motionless, as before, watching Sam. A full minute passed—an eternity. Sam's mind was spinning, tractionless ... stuck in the mud, going nowhere. He cleared his throat.

"So, what now?"

The ant remained immobile, watching. He cleared his throat again, trying to pitch his voice in as soft and non-threatening manner as possible.

"All right, ant ... I'm going to stand up, okay? I'm just..."

The ant lifted its foot from Tes, but without aggression this time. Appearing completely unconcerned, it turned its back to Sam and moved back over to the bookshelf.

It knows it has us. The thought that the ant might be intelligent enough to understand that sent chills down Sam's spine.

Studying the armored form, Sam stood up, making no sudden movements, and edged towards the backpack, inside which lay the decade-old grenade. The ant had stopped and was doing something in between the shelves. Sam edged closer. Tes twitched, and then rose. She'd transferred back—if she'd ever left at all.

The ant turned, and Sam froze, tempted to run to the backpack, but knowing what the result would be. Something was in the ant's jaws. Sam paused and blinked, stunned.

It moved towards him, in that same nonaggressive way, and placed a box labeled "Dutch Chocolate" at Sam's feet.

Sam was dumbfounded.

A moment passed; Sam continued to stare at the box. He couldn't believe what he was seeing.

"Open it, Samuel."

At the sound of Tes's voice, the ant's head whipped towards her, but it stayed put, standing over the box.

Sam crouched down, eyes never leaving the ant. The insect, appearing satisfied that Tes wasn't going to do anything, swung her enormous head back to Sam.

Sam sliced down the center of the box with his boot knife and opened a flap. Stacks of pristine chocolate bars—a hundred of them, if the number on the box was to be believed—lay stacked as though they'd been packed yesterday.

Years of eating and drinking only what he could scavenge from ants evoked an uncontrollable Pavlovian response. Before Sam could stop himself, he was ripping off the glistening wrapper of the bar, and sinking his teeth into the dark candy.

The world dimmed as the long-forgotten flavor exploded into his mouth.

Oh, wow...

The chocolate wiped away the near escape with the post-human. The ant, only a foot away from him, was gone. Pure joy, overwhelming ecstasy washed over him, as memories of better times came tumbling, unbidden. An abstract part of him was aware of tears streaming down his face, but he didn't care.

After a few moments, Sam managed to pull himself together, opening his eyes. The holographic wrappers of five chocolate bars were scattered around him. Tes stood like a protective guard dog between him and the ant, who was still staring at him placidly.

Sam reached out with trembling hands, shocked and embarrassed by his response, and laid them on the box.

"Thank you. I don't know if you understand me, but thank you."

The insect remained a statue.

"So … what now? What does this mean? Why did you come here?"

The ant opened its mouth, pincers spread wide. Sam flinched, even though he sensed no hostility. A small hiss escaped the ant's mouth, like faint static, and she snapped her pincers shut. It regarded Sam for a second and then turned around, heading back to the bookshelves, disappearing between them. Sam hesitated, unsure of what to do. Seconds passed.

Tes decided for him, scuttling between the tall shelves.

Sam lurched upright, feeling a strange detachment from his body and followed her.

"Over here, Samuel."

Sam followed the sound of her voice to the far back left corner of the Alamo. There he found her, standing over a hole about six feet wide. A thick, gooey mucous blocked the entire opening. Tes extended a leg, tapping it. Appearing to gain confidence, she eased herself onto the cover, which was hardening and thickening. A small sensor extended from her abdomen, inching down until it touched the substance.

"What is it, Tes?"

"One second. I am getting acoustics." A thin filament extended, pressing and twisting into the gel before Tes jerked free.

"This is an organic compound. Appears to be an ul-tra-dense crystalline matrix impregnated with a liposomally encapsulated acid. It's a seal, and anything that tries to break in will be eaten alive by the acid."

"Okay, what about the echo results?"

"Get your vision goggles and see for yourself. I'll keep pulsing to refine the image. The low-resolution feed-back I'm getting is pretty incredible," Tes said.

Sam scrambled back to the chair and found the goggles lying on the floor. He put them on, reattaching the goggles to the batteries in his vest. The screen blinked on, revealing the blue-green three-dimensional diagram of an echographic image. Sam could see the tunnel the ant had made, winding through the office building, ignoring walls, passing through his barriers, and—seeing it made chills go down his spine—weaving around his proximity mines and booby traps. The sonography showed the mucous plug in his floor was about three feet thick, with what looked like another plug at the entrance of the tunnel, which origi-nated in the foundations of the building. From there, the image lost resolution, but it was enough.

"*They* came from under the street, Tes. I say 'they' because there's no way a singular ant did this. This was pur-poseful. Intentional. They wanted to penetrate the Alamo, but why? Deliver me chocolate? That ant could have, should have killed me. I mean, I've been killing her colony mates for a decade! Tell me you've figured it out."

"No idea, Samuel. Insufficient data. What we do know is that the ant was not hostile. It knew what kind of food humans eat and brought some. It understood more than that, though, because it brought high-quality, well-preserved food. This intimates a level of intelligence we ha-ven't previously observed or suspected. Intentional intelli-gence."

"Okay, fine. So they're not going to kill us. What about the tunnel? We should fill it ... blow it in." Sam said.

"I disagree. Take another look. Those echographically bright blips every five yards? Those are our directional proximity mines. They moved them into the tunnel, and I suspect, if we were to go down there, we would find them aimed away from us, towards the street. They are protecting us, Samuel."

Sam sighed and pulled off the goggles.

"Okay, you win. There's nothing we can do anyways. They cut through our defenses like they weren't there. Filling the hole won't stop them. I can't think anymore. I'm hitting the sack."

"Great idea, Samuel. I'll review data logs. I'll wake you at eleven a.m."

"Why so late?"

"It is almost three in the morning. You know the rules. Eight hours of sleep for optimal performance and health."

"Oh, right. Okay. Good night."

Sam ducked into his bedroom, pulling the door behind him and locking it.

"Lock the door, Samuel."

"Locked. G'night, Tes."

I'll never be able to sleep after...

Sam was out before his head hit the pillow.

Morning came early or, rather, the abrasive strains of the New Philadelphia city anthem. Sam sat bolt upright, disoriented, until bit by bit the prior day's events came back to him, like scraps of a halfway remembered nightmare.

"Tes, what's up? What time is it?"

"Eleven a.m. The ants are back."

Sam scrambled in the darkness, bumping his head on a shelf in his haste to find the door.

"What?! Why didn't you wake me! I'm coming out! Is it safe to come out?"

"It is safe. You needed your eight hours of sleep, and I felt you were safer in the panic room until I ascertained their intentions."

Sam found the lock and threw the door open, squinting past the sunlight spilling in. Three ants stood in the middle of the room. The middle one appeared to be the same bull ant that had visited them before. On the floor in front of them lay three large sealed bags. Right away Sam recognized them: military-grade food rations. Each bag was a month of high-quality human food. The Pavlovian response rose again, and he fought to control himself.

"I think that they are saying this food is from an underground research center about eight miles away from here. Geographic locations are the easiest to understand. I am obtaining a lot of this from the food's data tags. The food is in perfect condition. I think something happened at the research center … a biologic mutagen failsafe mechanism was triggered or something. If they were following standard protocol, that would mean the air was sucked out of the complex, which was then sealed. I do not know. It is hard to parse her syntax and language structure. I am developing an algorithm to assemble it into a Western-human format."

"What?? You can understand them?"

"Yes. I only have twenty percent comprehension, though. Their language structure is quite intricate, fractal based. I am developing a second response algorithm, but my understanding of their language follows a logarithmic curve that gets exponentially more complex the closer to one hundred percent I get."

"I am so confused right now. How are you communicating?"

"Binary, a high compression ratio, delivered in bursts. Judging from the delivery format, I believe she somehow intercepted computer mainframe exchanges—perhaps wireless—and assumed it was the human language. Or at least, a version of human language she could mimic. Quite remarkable, actually. I have been combing my databases ... never seen anything like it."

The news forced the food's origins out of Sam's mind. He stared at the ants, wrestling with his incredulity. The constant surprises were fraying his nerves.

"She? Only one can talk?"

"No. She is the intelligence. The ants have a hive mind. Or at least, I believe they do, based on transmission patterns. She is the metamind, the intelligence that is using the ants to reach out to us."

One of the ants, the one who came the day before, opened its pincers and exhaled a brief static sound. She clicked her jaws shut and, in unison, all three ants turned around and filed into the bookshelves. Sam watched them go, struggling to process it all.

"Right before they left ... that hiss you heard. That was them ... her ... telling us they will be back here tomorrow, except the word for 'here' is an organic version of GPS, with this specific location," Tes said.

"So ... what do they want?"

"They did not say. Or perhaps they did, and I did not understand. As we speak, I am reviewing the interaction and trying to fill blank spots. It is almost like cracking data encryption ... a lot of brute force processing that is going to take hours."

Sam moved over to the bags the ants had left and crouched down to inspect them. The bags' holographic displays, still crisp, detailed the contents of each bag and a short, silent video on how to prepare its contents. Sam shook his head, touching them in disbelief. Once again, the ants had delivered food that looked like it had been made yesterday.

Sam accessed a bag's display, selected an option, and the bag unsealed. Sam pulled out a meal cube, inspecting it before taking a bite. The flavors of the food flooded into his mouth, causing his vision to blur from the sheer sensation of tasting food.

"We'd better ration this. Can you run an inventory and calculate a good balance between caloric consumption and making these last?" Sam's words were muffled through the mouthful of food.

"I can."

"Also, Tes. I think we should bury the hemolymph we took. Like, give it a proper burial. It's the least we can do."

Tes remained silent, and for a moment Sam thought she was going to disagree with him, until she flexed her manipulators—her way of nodding in agreement.

"I will see if I can get the borer up and running. What time tonight do you want to head out?"

"Let's do it now. I don't think the ants are a threat anymore. I'll start moving the sacks back down to the street. There's a spot about a hundred yards southwest of here that has a patch of bare earth we can dig into."

The rest of the day passed without incident, filled with hard labor that didn't allow much room for wild thinking. Afternoon turned into evening before they'd put earth over the last of the hemolymph sacks and made a simple memorial over it.

Sam was grateful to climb into the panic room that night and fell asleep before he could tell himself he was going to have a hard time falling asleep.

The next day, Sam awoke with a start, realizing he didn't hear Tes's patriotic alarm. Checking his watch, he saw it was eight in the morning. An hour before his official wake time. Sam eased himself over to the door and pressed his ear against it, straining to hear anything on the other side.

Seconds passed and then he heard a telltale hiss. After a pause, a second hiss.

He unlocked the door and stepped out. The same three ants were back, with more boxes of food in front of them but, this time, all their attention focused on Tes. The AI sat on top of the boxes, emitting a similar hiss.

"So, you can talk back?"

"No, not yet. Last night I realized that it is not only the binary content, but the delivery speed and compression ratio that communicates information. I am at twenty-eight percent comprehension right now, which is way better than I was projecting yesterday."

The ant in the middle, whom Sam was beginning to think of as the leader, hissed again, turned, and headed back to the floor exit behind the library, followed by the other ants.

"Get any of that?"

"From that exchange, only the words 'follow,' and 'die,' which they express as a genocide-level event. That's what makes this challenging. There's no consistency in their vocabulary. The same sounds can have different meanings if certain factors I am not aware of are modified. However, if I am understanding the context right, they told me they have been looking for you."

"So … when they said to follow, was it directed at us, or was the ant talking to another ant?"

"It is difficult to say, but given that the ant was speaking in the binary compression, I would say it was directed at us. If it was among themselves, I doubt they would communicate like that."

"Okay. So what happens if we do that, if they come back tomorrow? See where they are getting this food from? I thought about this a lot yesterday. The Alamo isn't safe anymore, Tes. They've proved they can compromise it at will. If they want us to follow them, maybe we should. They could have done it by force at any time."

"I am not sure that is wise, Samuel. This area is way more than just security. We can account for these new flaws. Restructure."

"No, I was thinking about this last night, too. If they come back, I want to go. Go into the tunnel with them. I want you to come in the droid. We need to see where they're getting that food. Whatever is protecting the food can also protect us."

"I still believe it is unwise to—"

"We're going, Tes. If nothing else, to see the size of this food cache. Have you looked at the air rifle? Is it fixable?"

"It is repairable." By design, artificial intelligences did not utilize emotions like anger or resentment, but sometimes Sam wondered.

"Okay, let's get to work then. Plan on a two-week expedition. I'm going to try to get the exoskeleton working—I don't think I'll be able to keep up with the ants without it, and you'll need to attach to something to not fry your body. May need to pull the fusion battery from the sensor pods."

"Fine." Her tone was flat.

Tes turned and moved over to the workshop, where he could see she was already working on repairing the air rifle. Once again, Sam got the feeling she was upset with him.

"Thanks, Tes..."

The AI pulled herself up onto workbench stool and settled down, her spider's legs gripping the lip of the seat. Selecting a tool hanging on the wall, she began to work, the only sound being the soft whine of her aging servos.

Sam decided to leave her alone, give her space. He went over to the storage bay and pulled the door open. After rummaging through containers and shelves, he found what he was looking for: a dark green jumpsuit made of a thick, almost muscular fabric.

He hauled it over to the workbench beside Tes, and they worked next to each other, side by side, for hours. The work absorbed Sam, and he lost track of time until the sound of Tes stowing the repaired gun in the exoskeleton's cargo backpack jolted him back to reality.

The work on the suit's power supply, which was right at the limit of his repair abilities, pulled him back in.

The day passed into night. Sam was hunched over a power distribution module, checking his repairs, when he realized Tes was talking to him.

"What did you say, Tes?"

"I said, 'Go to sleep.' The ants have been coming at eight a.m. It is eleven. You need your eight hours."

"Tes, this is one time when I think we can…"

"No. You have to sleep. I will finish the exoskeleton checks. It looks functional now," said Tes.

Sam knew better than to argue with her. Her perfect recall put him on the losing side every time. He stood, wincing at the soreness in his neck and arms.

"Fine. After that, we'll be ready. See you in the morning."

"Good night, Samuel."

Morning came too soon. Again, Sam was up before Tes's alarm, and after being chastised for not sleeping for eight hours, he put on the exoskeleton, testing it out. The muscular fabric tensed and flexed like new. Sam maneuvered in it around the room, while Tes followed like a nervous parent.

"Looks good. Battery is holding up under the load; I think the power redirection idea did the trick. Let's move everything over to the hole and wait," Sam said.

Sam munched on a chocolate bar as he grabbed the heavy cargo backpack and, with the exoskeleton's help, moved it over to the ants' entrance, placing it by the mucous plug. Tes came behind him, bringing his goggles and the rifle.

"Thanks for repairing that yesterday, Tes."

"It is functional. I reconsidered my position, and I have changed my mind. We should at least investigate this food source, in light of deficiencies here at the Alamo."

Below them, they heard a distant scrabbling sound emanating from beneath the plug.

"They're coming."

The membrane bulged, then ruptured in the middle, a pair of enormous pincers chewing through it. Sam watched as the ants removed the plug, appearing to eat it despite the acid vesicles. One by one they climbed out, until they were all standing uncomfortably close around the hole. Their smell was earthy, organic, much like the sponge from the nursing ants. The ants each carried another sealed bag of military rations in their pincers, which they deposited in a pile beside Sam. The leader hissed. After a moment, Tes hissed back.

"I am telling her we want to follow. At least, I believe I am."

The ants stood silent, regarding them with their enormous eyes. A moment passed.

"Tes, do you think maybe we should try to…"

One of the smaller ones stepped forward and picked up Tes. Another did the same with him, squeezing him as it lifted him in the air. The exoskeleton responded, hardening under the grip, but the ant's grip was gentle.

Without the hint of a warning, the ants plunged back into the tunnel, into pitch black. Unable to see, Sam tried to put the goggles on, but the ants were moving with frightening speed, throwing him all over the place. It was all he could do just to hang on to the rifle and the goggles as they twisted and turned. Sam got the sensation he was missing the edges of the tunnel by mere inches, and fought hard to not to let his imagination run wild.

I can't take much of this … we'd better get there soon.

Sound was muted by the earthen walls of the tunnel, with only the soft patter of the ants' movement. An unknown amount of time passed, and Sam tried to relax into it, attempting to keep from tensing his body. They continued to move at breakneck speed, but Sam couldn't tell if they were going up, down, left, or right. He had the sense they were in an enormous complex of tunnels. In his mind's eye, he imagined a huge network underneath the entire city.

They stopped, and Sam's head snapped back from the sudden deceleration. Pitch black. A soft hiss, and Tes's voice, pitched low, disturbed the quiet.

"Post-human. I think there may be one in the tunnel."

Sam took in a deep breath. Sure enough, entwined in the pungent, earthy smell of the tunnel was the distinct odor of rot. He heard a rustle—one of the ants moving away from the rest. Sam took the opportunity to slip on the helmet and twist the power wires together. The display flickered, glowed, then they started moving again, at the same frenetic pace.

It took a minute for Sam to orient himself because everything in the image blended in together. They were beginning to dip into solid bedrock—he could see that much, which meant they were deep underground. There was one ant ahead; he could see Tes every once in a while as the ant holding her lifted its head to avoid an obstacle or duck below an underhang. Every few yards, the tunnel branched off—sometimes four or five times, heading in all directions, including up and down. The ants appeared to choose their path at random, continuing to fly down the tunnel.

The clock in his goggles told him they'd been going for three hours, and had already traveled fifty-five miles; something he wouldn't have thought possible if he couldn't see their real-time speed.

Without warning, the first ant stopped, antennae waving. After a moment, another ant appeared in the distant tunnel, its antennae waving in a counter-response. They approached until their antennae were almost entwined, feeling each other.

The new ant turned, heading back in the direction it came, and the other two followed, moving more at a slower pace. The tunnel widened, until they emerged into an enormous chamber with fluid, pulsatile walls. Sam frowned, adjusted his goggles, then realized the walls were actually ants—innumerable ants, swarming inside the cavern. At an area towards the middle of the chamber, the ants seemed to be forced back by an invisible barrier, swarming all around it, but never crossing an unseen line. Sam became aware of the sound of ceaseless insectoid movement—legs, carapaces, and bodies crawling and scrabbling over one another. In the center lay the biggest ant Sam had ever seen: thirty or more feet long, with enormous gossamer wings.

"The queen: I think she is hurt." Tes's voice was muffled.

The ants approached the clearing, and Sam refocused the image. He couldn't put his finger on it, but he knew Tes was right. The queen was limp, and as they drew closer, Sam realized her legs were twitched weakly, as though convulsing. With each twitch, the rest of the ants moved, twitching in the same way, each time she did.

They broke through the edge of the ant swarm, stepping into the clearing. The ant carrying Sam set him down in front of the queen.

Complete silence cut off the rustling like a knife the moment his feet touched the ground, hitting Sam like a punch. He looked around, saw every ant frozen in place, watching him. More ants piled in, standing on top of other ants, filling in until the tunnel entrances were below the sea of bodies, leaving only a column of space around them and the queen.

"Hive mind, Samuel. I think she is collecting herself to communicate."

The massed ants' antennae waved, vibrating faster and faster, until a low, physical thrum filled the room. The queen moved, shifting herself, bringing her enormous head around to look at them. She opened her pincers and hissed. Immediately, the ants went silent. A moment passed, and Sam felt like they were waiting for something—a response.

The queen hissed again.

"She wants me to approach her, Samuel."

Tes moved in underneath the giant ant. The queen lowered her head, caressing Tes with an antenna. Tes went stiff, a single leg twitching, imitating the queen.

"I have been looking for you. We have been looking for you. You are the last of your kind here. No others. We need you. Let me show."

The words poured out of Tes, as though they were being spoken by someone who didn't know how to formulate words.

"Let me show. I hurt. Our hive dies. You help. Our hive dies. Let me show."

A nudge from behind pushed Sam forward. Another nudge came, and another, until he was standing next to Tes. He looked to see who'd pushed, but there was no one there. He unfastened his goggles, shoving them off and letting them drop before he realized, with a great deal of surprise, that he had no control over what he was doing. The queen's other antenna came down, touching the center of his forehead.

Sam blacked out, but he felt something holding him up. Visions flashed before him, sounds, smells, thoughts, all alien and incomprehensible. They crowded in, pushing at his own sense of self, until he was washed away in the torrent of what the queen was pumping into his mind.

It was a mind-crushing blur of insanity, until, as though something had clicked into place, comprehension flooded through him and he *changed*.

Sam grew thin, oozed out, felt himself connect with every ant in the chamber until his mind was *her* mind, spread across innumerable ant minds, each contributing to a small part of her consciousness. Still, his awareness spread, like a ripple in a pool, expanding outward until distance and numbers became abstract concepts. He became aware of her enormous pain.

What...?

At the edge of her consciousness, he felt parts of her winking out, sometimes a single one, other times in bunches. Each one felt like a tiny light going dark, and each time he felt her consciousness, her intelligence, dim an almost imperceptible shade more. An enormous draw sucked Sam's mind towards that darkening area of herself. It enlarged, coming into focus, until he was *there.*

But he didn't know where *there* was. Once again a disorienting array of sights, sounds, and smells hit him, but he adapted much faster this time. Sam realized he was experiencing the sensation of dozens of ants all at once. His mind struggled to understand what he was viewing. As his mind started to tolerate the sensory overload, he began to see a liquid, moving view of an enormous post-human. It was much like the one that had almost got him, except he saw it from every angle, from the perspective of every ant surrounding it. The ants were in a pitched battle, throwing themselves at it, trying to tear it to pieces too small to reformulate.

Instinctively, Sam knew that the ants were trying to prevent it from pushing into their territory, where a nursery lay vulnerable, only a few hundred yards away.

The post-human ripped one of the ants in half, throwing the body in two different directions. Sam felt a small twinge of pain, then the queen ant's presence dimmed again, as the ant died.

The view shifted, pulling back, blowing up until Sam could feel and see through every ant in the colony. It was too much. He vomited, but he was too detached from himself to care as a dozen other similar battles being played out, like dark tumors in the network of the ant hive mind.

Please help me.

The words were plain as day, but given in a series of images and pheromones, touches, and postures.

We are losing to it. It knows. It hungers for me. You are the last of your kind here. Your kind's time is over. This is either our world or its world. You are the key. You are compatible. You can help. Please.

Sam could see, through the eyes of ants spread through a network that spanned most of the globe, that she was right. He was the only human left alive.

Except.

Sam focused in on what felt like a blind spot, a lack of awareness in the hive mind. He frowned mentally, not understanding. He shifted his view, realizing that the queen was observing him.

The random pieces clicked together. The blind spot was shaped like South America. The crazy stories of the man with the tiger tattoo came flooding back.

What about there? Why aren't you there?

Sam felt the ant queen respond to the inquiry, but the emotion was alien.

We cannot go in there. Neither can The Enemy.

Frustrated, Sam tried again. *What is in there? Are there humans?*

We cannot go in there. Neither can The Enemy. Will you help? Will you help?

Sam hesitated, not knowing what help meant. The queen—the colony—waited. He felt her weaken once again. Sam knew there wasn't a true choice anymore.

Yes. I will help.

With that, he was back in his own body. Sam felt his own physical limitations and lack of awareness compress him as immense claustrophobia overcame him. The room swam, and when he blacked out, this time, his consciousness went with him.

****

"Wake up, Samuel."

The voice in his ear was familiar, although he couldn't quite place it.

"Wake up, Samuel."

Sam opened his eyes into blinding light. He jumped up, unsure of what happened. He was standing in a small room (*no, a cave*) packed with ten ants, all staring at him. At his feet, Tes looked up at him, a small floodlight aimed at his face, giving everything an unearthly quality.

"Tes, where the heck are we?"

"We left New Philadelphia territory, but I cannot say with any precision. A lot of weird interference. The ants are saying you are supposed to follow them."

As though they understood, the ants turned, leading them outside. The sun was pale and weak, filtering through the greasy atmosphere. Sam saw they had come out of a squat house, one in a row of decaying structures.

"The ants say you are here to infect a post-human named New York."

"What?"

"I'm just relaying their message. Sounds weird to me, too. Listen, Samuel. Whatever happens, I want you to be careful. I ... you just need to stay safe, okay?"

"Okay, I will." Tes's tone unnerved Sam more than their strange situation.

One of the ants stepped forward. She was a huge specimen, her eyes level with Sam's. In her pincers was a small moving piece of meat. Sam recoiled.

"What is that?! Why does she have that chunk of a post-human?"

Before he could react, the ant moved forward, pressing the piece of moving tissue onto his neck. Sam jumped back, reaching up, but he was too slow. The disgusting filth buried into his skin, burrowing bony hooks deep into his neck. He tried pulling it off, but the thing sent gouts of pain shooting down his spine every time he touched it.

"TES? WHAT IS THIS?? TELL THEM TO TAKE IT OFF!!"

"I'm sorry, Samuel ... They didn't tell me about that. Wait ... okay, they say you need that so New York does not detect you."

"What the heck is New York?"

One of the ants hissed, then turned, going around a corner.

"It says to follow," Tes said.

"I don't like this."

Feeling like he didn't have a choice, Sam followed Tes around the house.

Shock.

Complete, overwhelming, shock.

Sam fell to his knees.

Off in the distance, about half a mile away, towering over everything and reaching into the clouds, was a giant wall of flesh, extending as far as the eye could see. Even from where he was, Sam saw countless individual humans fused into it, heard the faint screams of countless throats. Drops of the thing peeled off like beads of sweat, tumbling down and reforming into the creatures Sam had seen going through the streets of New Philadelphia for decades.

"What ... what is that, Tes?"

"I think that's New York."

"This ... that thing is alive?"

"More than that. Aware. The queen gave me access to sensory databases for the last twenty years ... every sensor for the entire city-state. While we were in that chamber, I watched it all. Watched it congeal. Over time, every post-human scrap has been collecting here, creating a kind of anti-consciousness to what the ants have. They are two intelligences, Samuel, fighting for control of the new Earth. The winner inherits it; the loser goes extinct. And the post-humans are winning."

"So what does that mean, Tes? What do they want me to do?"

"They want you to fuse with it, Samuel. The queen, when she touched you, she changed something about you. You're a host, a Trojan horse carrying something that she wants to infect New York with."

"If I do this, there isn't any coming back, is there?"

"No, Samuel."

A billion reasons he should refuse flooded into Sam's mind, screaming for his attention. Sam paused, and remembered the ants' desperate helplessness as their consciousness weakened in the face of the continual post-human onslaught. Genocide, one that only he could prevent.

"Okay, I'll do it."

The ants stirred, sensing his response.

"Under one condition."

They paused. Sam turned, facing them.

"I want you to take Tes to the edge of that blind spot in your awareness. To South America. I want you to leave her at the border … take her as far as you can. There are humans there. I don't care what you say, I know some of us survived. AIs need social interaction, or they go insane, and she will find someone there, someone who will be her companion."

The ants hissed, one after the other.

"They agree. I'm not doing that, though, Sam. I'm going with you. Into New York."

"You know you can't, Tes. Don't kid yourself. Let them take you. Find someone new. Keep yourself sane, so there is a record of all this."

Tes stayed quiet, her black spider's body drawn inward like a small child with her knees pulled to their chest.

"I don't like this, Sam." Sam noticed she'd stopped calling him Samuel. Somehow, that wasn't making things easier.

"I don't either, Tes. But I like the post-humans even less. No more talking. Let's do this, or I will chicken out."

Sam unhooked the backpack from the exoskeleton, letting it fall to the ground. Turning to the ants, he stared into their multifaceted eyes, trying to get past their alien features to the consciousness behind them. Emotion choked him, making his throat ache.

"You take her. You make sure she finds someone." He was going to say more, but couldn't. He had always been terrible with goodbyes, and was even worse now that it had been a couple decades since the last.

Feeling awkward, Sam turned, taking a step towards the mass in the distance.

"Sam…"

Sam paused, unable to turn around.

"I love you, Sam. I won't forget this. You. Ever."

He couldn't look at her.

"Goodbye."

Fighting his desire to call it all off, Sam started walking again, focusing on putting one foot in front of the other. There was no more fear, no more questions, no more uncertainty. Left foot, right foot, at a steady pace, keeping his eyes on the road ahead. Despite the temptation, he refused to look at the writhing bulk waiting for him.

About a hundred yards out, the stench became almost unbearable. Sam stripped off the exoskeleton and removed his shirt, wrapping it around his nose and mouth. It did little to help, but it was enough to keep him moving.

Fifty yards. Forgetting for a moment, Sam looked up and saw the fused cancer of tens of thousands of humans, all melted into one horrific nightmare. Fear blossomed, and he looked down at his feet, refocusing on walking.

Twenty-five yards. Something brushed past him, leaving a thick smear of skin. Sam's chest was about to burst from holding back the scream and, with effort, he refocused on the path in front of him.

Five yards. He couldn't see. The stench was causing the air to waver like a mirage. He vomited into the shirt. Disgusted, he ripped it off, throwing it into the ground.

One yard. Finally, there was no avoiding it. Nowhere to look where the post-human wasn't. He moved closer, until his feet were almost touching the edge. Rivulets of pus leaked down the wall of moaning flesh, trickling to the ground and around his feet.

Sam didn't stop to think about it. Without looking up, he reached out, touching the mass in front of him.

He felt slick, feverish skin underneath his fingers and pressed harder, pushing with both hands.

The wall responded, shooting enormous barbs through the palms of his hands. The barbs punched through Sam's arms, erupting out his back. Sam tried to scream, but the indescribable pain took his breath away.

A flash of panic flooded his body as the barbs contracted, pulling him into the post-human's bulk. Flesh filled his mouth, nose, throat, down into his lungs, everything. Sam panicked, trying to fight, but it was too late. The post-human mass opened up to consume him, assimilating him.

Wrong, the ants were wrong … there's nothing I can—

The thing on his neck shifted, tunneled deeper, inserting a pseudopod into his brain even as his body began to melt.

What—

Something in his mind switched on, and New York froze.

Sam saw himself, floating on the edge of the post-human. Saw his brain, now wired into the massive creature through the thing the ant had placed on his neck. His point of view shifted, blurring, spinning out of control until, without warning, it stopped. And he was himself again.

Except his body was now New York, with thousands of pieces of himself spreading all over the world, everywhere except to the same South-American-shaped blind spot. Just like the ants, the post-human was a giant hive mind, comprised of all the human dead it had harvested. He could feel the malignant consciousness of the post-human struggling against him, trying to regain control.

Regain control...

Realization flooded through him.

I am in control.

New York, the hive consciousness, tore at Sam's invading mind, wrestling for peripheral control. In the few seconds that had passed, Sam realized he'd already lost about a third of the post-human.

Not much time.

He looked outside himself, outside of New York, detaching pieces and sending them running … looking.

He found the ants where he'd left them. Tes was with them. They'd formed a protective barrier around her, facing the post-human he was controlling. Sam stopped the post-human a few feet away. He tapped into the vast neural network of the post-human, concentrating.

Half a mile away, in front of the ants, a young red-headed girl lodged in the thigh of the post-human opened her mouth and hissed.

The ants hissed back, in unison.

Message received. We will honor our promise to you. We will see Tes to the edge of the dark zone.

An old sadness washed over Sam as he remembered his air rifle. Remembered how he'd bought it because he was afraid he'd use a real gun on himself.

I guess, somehow, I always knew I would.

He frowned internally, remembering a part of the Word he'd memorized years before.

No, this is different. Giving your life isn't the same as taking it. Greater love has no man than he who lays down his life for another.

He took a deep mental breath, steeling nerves that were no longer his own. The post-human consciousness' frantic struggles increased as it sensed what Sam was about to do.

It began as a single cell, turning on its neighbor. A small, almost undiscernible beginning, located where Sam's body floated in the mass. Sam watched as it grew, until, in seconds, it was raging, out of control, unstoppable, speeding through the post-human. Swathes of black appeared in his awareness. He felt his grip slipping, but he could also feel the post-human slipping too, growing dimmer with each passing moment. His consciousness narrowed, darkening alongside the creature, but he didn't care anymore.

Just one more thing he had to do. Had to say.

Half a mile away, the artificial intelligence called Tes watched as a mottled black necrosis crept across the enormous mass of New York's human flesh. Hours passed, and neither she nor the ants moved, watching as the creature decayed in front of them. The post-human Sam had sent stayed frozen in place, a million spasms wracking its body as its brain died.

Tes focused on New York and ignored a thump as the thing finally collapsed, unable to hold itself upright anymore.

"Tes..."

Startled, Tes swiveled to look at the post-human, a crumpled heap on the ground. The young redhead on the post-human's thigh was looking at her with weak eyes.

"Sam!"

"Tes ... I did it. It's dying. I can't see anymore. Can't hear, so I don't know if you're getting this ... but ... I should have told you when I left. I love you too."

"Sam..."

The redhead's face went slack. In the distance, a billion windpipes cried out at once, and then: silence.

ACT 3

RESURRECTION

Distant shouts, echoing down the mine shaft told Oosam his time was up—they had discovered him. No more delaying. He had to pull the brain out now, or lose the prize and face punishment for digging an illegal tunnel. If he laid hands on it and melded, he could force the miner's guild to use him if they wanted access to the brain of the god.

Oosam took in a deep breath, steeling his nerves as he studied the hard rock in front of him. The giant bones and organs of the dead god jutted out from the wall, harder than iron, yet flaking and peeling after thousands of years buried in the graveyard. It had taken Oosam a week to find the head, buried inside the alien-looking ribs of the god. It took another week of diligent, ginger excavation to expose the brain. A gray powder of crushed stone covered it, but it glistened at him in the flickering torchlight.

He ungloved his right hand and reached out, hesitating an inch away from the mottled sphere, unsure.

The shouts grew closer, and Oosam panicked, jerking his hand back, knocking into a rib. The brain, already loose in its skull, rolled forward, touching his exposed arm. Oosam took in a sharp breath, fear overwhelming him.

Nothing happened. Oosam smiled, greed-laced hope growing in him. He was alive! The god-brain had—

The thought choked off as his arm swelled, turning green, the skin splitting open where it was touching the brain.

Oosam started screaming, thrashing, trying to pull himself away, but his muscles had frozen, refusing to obey, preventing him from pulling back. His screams turned to shrieks, high pitched and frantic as the swelling crawled up his arm and down his torso, consuming his body.

On the other side of the tunnel, the crew searching for Oosam stopped at the sound of the inhuman cries.

"What is that? A daemon come breakin' tru our wards?" The voice of the searcher was shaky.

"Nae. He touched a god. Nothin' ta do but wait. We'll seal this off inna case somethin' leaks out," said the foreman. He was a short man with a chronic hunch from a lifetime under the low rock ceilings of the mine. No one in the group protested—they all knew what that scream could mean for anyone who went down the tunnel.

"Gaath, blow tha entrance. Just enough ta bury it. We'll have ta open it up again, and we don't need extra work."

The miners worked fast, setting up a small blast charge at the mouth of Oosam's tunnel as his screams continued to reverberate off the stone walls. Without ceremony, the foreman blew the opening, bringing down part of the ceiling. As the thick dust settled, he raised his hand for silence, and the men listened for any sound.

After a moment, they could hear Oosam again, but the wailing was so quiet it sounded almost imaginary.

"Good enough. We'll come back in three days, if the council gives its blessing."

Butcher Block Green

The crew returned to the mining base in Auburn to wait for the time of cleansing to elapse. Rumors swirled in the villages and mining camps about Oosam, and what he might have found. Whispered gossip grew that the miner had been careless—greedy, trying to hoard a dead god's brain for himself. The scandal of it—trying to handle a god without a witcher—fueled a palpable excitement that permeated every conversation among the townsfolk. Auburn was an isolated wasteland town, with strong wards that protected villagers from predators, so little ever happened. After three days, the excitement was at a fever pitch when the miners hauled Oosam's swollen, lacerated body out of the mineshaft. The townsfolk treated the retrieval team like heroes as they marched back to the mine, encumbered by thick protective gear covered in protective brands and wards. It didn't last long. Upon entering the shaft, twin brothers Daanso and Liisan fell ill, their bodies swelling and splitting open just like Oosan's. The rest of the retrieval team abandoned them, still alive, and resealed the mine.

There was a raging debate whether to just collapse the tunnel and leave everything there. Three years prior, another miner had died in much the same way. When they'd tried to remove his body, the ones who'd touched him had been stricken with a terrible disease. The fear of another plague was the focal point of countless shouting matches in the weekly city council meetings. The dead god's brain was too valuable to leave, but no one was willing to risk it. After two days of voting, the council sent an orphan boy to Auburn's witcher, who inscribed him with the necessary wards and sent him down the tunnel as a test. The town waited, everyday routines tinged with excited anticipation for the god-brain and the potential wealth it would bring. Three days after putting the boy underground, the horns sounded. The orphan had emerged unscathed, the god-brain held in his thin arms.

The news spread like a locust infestation: the body was coming up from the mine! The dusty streets turned into a festival ground as people from surrounding villages poured in. Some wanted a glimpse of the new god, and some were just hoping for free food and beer. Laughter, shouts, and the occasional fight broke out as people crushed together along the road, waiting for the mining team.

The warbled droning of the skdriitt pipes heralded the arrival of the party from the mine. The noise in the streets quieted as people jostled for a good view of the dead god's brain. No one dared get too close, just in case the god awoke and decided to punish them. Fluttering wards, colors long dulled by the sun, wafted above the procession as it moved down the street, protecting the mining party as it brought the brain to the revival witcher. The orphan boy came first, holding the mottled sphere aloft. Behind him came a dog cart hauling Oosam's naked body, a not-so-subtle reminder to the village about the consequences of mining for dead gods without the blessing of the village and the protection of the witchers. The mining chief and town officials came next, each wearing the blue and purple robes of their office. Finally, the unfortunate twins, Daanso and Liisan, bounced along in a wagon, wrapped in clean burial cloth. Green fluid dripped down the cart onto the brown dust of the road, trailing back to the mine.

The procession moved through town, to the outskirts. Villagers fell in line behind them, singing, laughing, and drinking. This was the first god-brain discovered in years. In recent months, there had been quiet, urgent whispers that perhaps the Auburn mine would be closed. It was an omen, people said. Good fortune was around the corner, as long as the god would awaken.

The noisy cavalcade reached the edge of the town, and the group halted. Encircling the town were its wards: totems and sigils that protected its inhabitants from any negative consequences of reanimating a god. The crowd waited at the edge, along with the town officials, watching as the mining chief, orphan, and two ward-bearers made their way to a stone building half a kilometer distant.

The orphan's arms trembled with the weight of the god, but the chief was nervous now that they'd passed beyond the safety of the sigils, and picked up his pace.

"Hurry, boy. Don't drop it. I don't want to spend any more time out here than I have to."

The boy jogged to keep up with the big man's steps, and soon the two halted in front of the witcher's dome, where the revival witcher stood waiting. He was a young man, tattooed and cauterized with the cryptographic runes and formulae of the ancients. He'd just inherited the position from his father, who was dying from the effects of too much time in the presence of the dead gods, and therefore unable to hold the office.

The mine chief cleared his throat nervously. He was also new; his predecessor had died in a tunnel collapse accident a few weeks prior.

"Witcher Thaame, the town presents this god to you. As laid out in our charter articles, we, the leadership of Auburn, authorize you to revive the deity, within the guidelines of your order, for the benefit and prosperity of our town. As per the articles, we will offer no intervention if you are injured, no aid if you fail. As per the articles, you get the witcher's fifth if you succeed. Do you accept the charge?"

The young man bowed his runed head and ran both hands across his face, tracing the scars of sigils there, loosening their power.

"I accept the charge. Give me the boy and the god. Set the watch at the limits of the town."

The mining chief shoved the orphan towards the witcher and backed away a little too fast.

"Advise the town of the acceptance."

The two ward-bearers turned, raising their flags. The breeze picked up the faded fabric, snapping it straight, and they began waving in an intricate pattern. The mining chief watched, impatient.

ERIC KRAMER

At the edge of town, villagers wheeled defensive explosives into place, arming them. After completing the delicate task, signal flags went up, etching a reply in the hot sky. If something went awry, the watchers would blow the witcher dome sky high.

The thought made the mining chief more nervous. He turned, half-jogging back to the wards protecting the town, the two ward-bearers struggling to keep up behind him.

The witcher watched them go, a strange expression on his face. After a moment he turned to the boy, inspecting him.

"What's your name?" Thaame asked.

"Saat, sir."

"Well. How old are you?"

"Twelve, sir. I think. Someone once told me I was older, but I think I'm twelve."

"Call me Thaame, Saat. Let's go inside, it's hot out. Here, give me that."

The witcher grabbed the brain, startling Saat, and went inside the dome. Saat hesitated before following him into the cool shade, where he found the witcher placing the god's brain on a large altar that stood in the middle of the darkened room. He watched as the witcher applied different patches, cables—unidentifiable totems of the ancients.

"How long were you in the mines with the brain?"

"They told me it was for a little over two days, sir … Thaame."

"And?"

"And what?"

"Did it try to talk to you? Try to move? Anything?"

"No, sir. It's dead. How could it talk?"

"These aren't dead. They're just … well, they're older than anything you can think of, and time makes them go insane. That is, until they go to sleep. Usually, only a witcher can wake them up, but it sounds like that idiot Oosam actually managed to do it, even if it was just for a

84

moment. Even then, it appears to have been just a reflex. Which is good, because it's better than trying to revive a dead…"

The witcher drifted off mid-sentence, focusing on his work. His hands flickered around the brain, making deft, birdlike movements over a convoluted nest of wires and cables. Every once in a while, a hand would flit up to rub one of the sigils on his head, as if drawing power from it. An hour passed, and the tattooed man continued to work, ignoring Saat, who was happy to just stand there and watch.

A soft beep from a glowing parchment disrupted the silence, catching the witcher's eye. He inspected it, grunting in approval. Saat shifted, trying to get a view of what was on the parchment, and accidentally sent an iron rod crashing to the floor. The witcher started, as if he'd forgotten anyone was with him. He stared at Saat as though he'd never seen the boy. Saat shifted under the strange man's gaze, unable to look into the sunken eyes. The silence stretched out.

"Saat, how long did you touch it for, while you were in the mines?"

Saat flinched, and then realized he wasn't going to get hit.

"The entire two days, as I was commanded."

"Are you sure? You didn't stop touching it once? Even for a few seconds to go to the bathroom?"

"No, sir … Thaame."

"And you're sure you touched it. I mean, you aren't lying to me. It's understandable if you are. You were in the dark for two days with the corpse of someone who touched it. I wouldn't blame you if…"

"I held my left hand on it until the moment you took it, sir."

Thaame looked at Saat with that same piercing look. Saat glared back, now unafraid.

"All right, then. Come over here. This will only hurt a little."

Thaame led Saat over to the altar and pulled out a cable with a round circle covered in a soft fuzz.

"Turn around. Bend your head down."

The witcher grabbed Saat's head, a sigil-callused hand forcing Saat's chin to his chest. Tufts of black hair began wafting down onto his bony shoulders as the witcher shaved his head.

"This is going to burn, but don't move."

Cold steel pressed into Saat's skull. Liquid warmth spread around from behind, reaching his ears. Saat forced himself to remain motionless, unwilling to show fear. Whatever was on his skull emitted a small, high-pitched whine and his head exploded in pain. An involuntary moan escaped his lips as the thing bored into his head, the vibrations jarring his whole skull. The witcher pressed harder, twisting, and Saat felt a small pop right inside his brain. The witcher let him go and walked over to his nest of wires and tools. Through the fog of pain, he heard Thaame talking to him, and Saat struggled to focus.

"… will take the implant a few minutes to connect to your own brain. You might see, hear, taste, or feel strange things. You will have a fairly painful headache the next few days, but not to worry. All of that will go away once we remove you from your mind and insert the god inside. This is quite the find. The god-brain appears to have no damage or rot."

Thaame walked back over carrying a long rod connected to a rat's nest of different colored cables. He gripped Saat's head with an iron hand, forcing his head forward.

"Now, you need to hold still. If you move, this will go too far inside, and we'll have to bind someone else to the god-brain."

Saat's vision flared, and he vomited.

Pain shot through his skull, and the taste of cooked meat filled his mouth. The scent of fresh figs came and went. Thousands of flies swarmed him, covering his skin, crawling all over him. Saat lashed out scratching and slapping, trying to get them away.

"Stop fidgeting! You're going to ruin the connection!"

A heavy smell of smoke filled his nostrils. Saat gagged, stomach heaving. He became aware he was on the floor, unable to control his spasming muscles, and that he'd lost control of his bowels.

Thaame squatted down next to him, studying the strange symbols of the ancients scrolling across the glowing parchment. He touched something on it, and Saat's body went rigid. Another touch, and it relaxed, every muscle trembling. Thaame reached behind Saat's head and unplugged the cable, leaving a rough metal square in the base of his skull.

"You're connected. Before we go further, I'm required to say that the town thanks you for your sacrifice, and you will be remembered in the list of the willing. Not that you had a choice, I imagine. One more thing, and we are ready. Lie down on your stomach. I have to place something in your back."

"I don't want to! I don't want to do this!" Saat's voice was trembling, weak.

The witcher seemed unsurprised. He touched the sigils on his face, mumbling to himself, tracing the scars, and then touched something on his glowing parchment. Saat went limp, unable to move his body. The witcher flipped him and cut his shirt off. Cold instruments touched Saat's back for a second, then pulled away. The room was quiet save for the sounds of metal instruments clanking against each other—sounds that frightened him. A sharp pain blossomed between his shoulder blades, right over his spine.

Saat tried to scream, but all he could do was make weak, breathless cries. His lungs didn't seem to be able to take in a deep breath, leaving Saat hungry for air. The witcher worked on, uncaring. More things pressed on Saat's back, tools that caused electricity and numbness to shoot down his limbs. The pain turned time into an eternity as exhaustion turned the boy's cries turned into whimpers, his head buried in his arms. The witcher ignored it all, continuing to work, placing something heavy along Saat's spine. A series of clicks accompanied a thousand sharp needle pricks along Saat's back. He shouted, tried to jump, but remained paralyzed, glued to the floor.

"Done." A soft sound from the glowing parchment, and Saat could move again. The strange weakness lifted off his chest. Saat took a huge breath in and let it out. Tears streamed down his face, and although he fought to hold it back, Saat started crying. Thaame seemed not to notice, but started speaking to him as though nothing were wrong.

"I've mounted the brain in your back, or rather mounted it in a device that will power it and allow it to communicate. The device is slaved into your spinal cord and blood vessels ... that's how it communicates and powers itself. After a couple weeks, it will overwhelm your body, and you'll die. Before that happens, over the next few days, we'll wake up the god, move it into your brain, and extract all the information we can."

Something flew across Saat's eye, a hovering image. He swatted at it, but his hand passed right through.

"There is a cot over there. Go lie down. Lie on your side ... the brain is in your back, so you can't lie flat."

An explosion rocked the witcher's dome, blasting debris and dust past them. Startled, Thaame jumped up, racing to the door. He reached for the handle, and the door blew open, knocking him back in a ball of fire and smoke. Saat scrambled behind the altar, hidden in the thick cloud of dust hanging in the air.

Through the dust he saw the witcher sitting up, holding his head. Dark blood oozed from it, dust sticking to the wound. The witcher touched his sigils and scars, moving his hands in ritualistic patterns. Saat hunched lower, unsure of what to do.

Butcher Block Green

In the doorway, an apparition appeared, loose shadows oozing off it, fluttering in the wind. The witcher still sat, rubbing his sigils. Dust congealed around him, twisting in gnarled knots. The shadow at the door saw it and gave a shout, running towards the witcher.

Thaame froze, a single finger tapping a sigil on his forehead. The sand around him condensed into a solid column, driving forward with blinding speed, slamming into the oncoming figure. The wall of the witcher's dome exploded as the column of sand punched through the apparition and blew out the wall behind it.

The witcher stood, still rubbing his sigils, his hands now tracing down his neck, shoulders, and chest. Saat watched, terrified, as the witcher's legs and arms began to thicken, elongate. Thaame's head remolded, bone erupting from his sigils with liquid pops and crawling down across his face like a giant spider, covering his eyes, nose, and mouth.

Outside the witcher's dome, shouts and more explosions rolled in through the doorway.

"I want you to stay out of this, boy. Whatever happens, you protect that god-brain. If you die before it awakens, we will not be able to recover it, and your soul will be forfeit," said Thaame's voice, muffled behind his bone mask.

The witcher took a step towards the doorway, the building shook, and everything disintegrated in fire.

****

Saat awoke to the sounds of distant screams and shouts. His head was ringing, echoing the smell of superheated blood and crack of weapons like a gong inside his skull. A white powder filled his mouth, eyes, and nose. He coughed, spitting out wet clots of dust.

The vision in his right eye flickered, and he felt his right arm move. Startled, Saat looked down and saw an odd liquid latticework tracing over his skin. He touched it, gingerly. It was hard as iron, but when he flexed his arm, it appeared to flex with him.

An explosion rocked the desert, sending melting globs of sand zipping past him. A few stung his face and arms, burning welts into him. Through the haze of sand and smoke, the witcher moved like a whirlwind, chanting oral wards in an ancient tongue. The man's sigils had taken over his entire body, snaking out of his skin and taking on a life of their own. Three dark shapes were on him, swinging weighted battle-blades with brutal violence, trying to find an opening, but it was like fighting smoke. Thaame was a blur, dancing around his attackers with impossible speed, with greater fluidity than human joints should allow. Thick spears of sand whipped around him, glistening in the heat of the midday sun like oiled serpents, breaking and reforming around the battle-blades. One of the sand spears found an opening, darting out like a lizard's tongue and skewering a figure. A mist of blood and sand exploded out of the man's—or daemon's—back, and it collapsed.

Beyond the frantic battle, an oily black smoke rose up from the town. Deep horns sounded. Saat's heart stopped in his throat as he recognized the necrotic tones twining together, announcing the fall of the town.

Raiders. Oh no … Quuin!

TTTThuTTTTTINITIATE::::

The sound pounded into his brain as though someone was inside his ears yelling at him. He understood every strange letter and symbol, even though he'd never heard or seen them before.

TTTThuTTTTTINITIATE::::

This time, it didn't hurt. Off in the distance, one of the raiders, a giant as big as the witcher, swung low with a huge blade, slicing off one of Thaame's legs. The witcher went down, sand spears writhing.

"AAAAAIIIAAAAAIIIAAA!"

The scream was raw agony, right into his brain. It came from inside him—from that thing on his back. The sound cascaded like molten lead down every nerve in his body, coming to a focal point at the thing on his back. Saat blacked out, but managed to stay conscious. After a moment, his vision returned.

::ERROR::ERROR::

::CHRYSALIS_WEAPON_AI::BAD::SEC-TORS.653.123.4.45::

The sensation pounded into his brain. Saat squinted, shook his head, trying to focus on what was in front of him. One of the raiders was standing over Thaame, bringing an enormous spiked hammer down onto the witcher's head. A shout, and the raider looked up, right at Saat.

His mind was on fire. Nothing seemed real. Saat stood and started running. He didn't move anywhere. Confused, he looked down and realized he wasn't standing.

What is going on??

He stood up. After a second's delay, his legs obeyed, as though they were operating a second behind his mind. He took a step forward. A second later his leg obeyed, and he moved. Saat almost toppled over. He tried again, and again. It was getting easier. The raider was walking to him, enormous battle blade gripped in a giant hand. A thick, painted mud mask hid the man's features, except for his dark eyes, with red fluid leaking out under them.

::CHRYSALIS_WEAPON_AI::REINITIATE::

::CHRYSALIS_WEAPON_AI::ACCESS-ING::STORED::PERSONALITY::

"EEEEEEEEEEEEEEHIAAAAAAA"

Saat had taken four steps when the same scream ripped through his head, brought him down—as effective as a blow to the head. Saat moaned, and tried to turn over, but a huge mass on his back prevented him from rolling farther than his side.

::ERROR::ERROR::BAD::SECTORS::

::CHRYSALIS_WEAPON_AI::PARTITION::COM-
PLETE::

::CHRYSALIS_WEAPON_AI::REINITIATE::

Each word stabbed at his brain, arcing down his spine. Needing to get away, Saat jumped up, stumbling, running. More shouts echoed behind him, coming his way. Ahead lay the black-veined wasteland that leached in from the dead ocean, but he didn't care.

"Why are you running?"

Saat jolted at the voice. It came from the center of his head, crystal clear in the desert air. Frantic, he looked around, his hands covering his head. Behind him, two of the raiders were running after him, huge blades flashing in the late afternoon sun. A third one knelt in the sand, working on something. He raised the thing to his shoulder, aiming it at Saat.

"Why are you running?"

"Those … those raiders are going to kill me." Saat gasped, in between ragged breaths. Behind him, a low crack rippled across the sand, and Saat risked another glance back. A blur streaked over the pursuing raiders, arcing towards him.

"They have fired at you. I am tracking it. Would you like me to respond?"

"What? Respond? What do you mean? Who are you? Where are you?"

Ahead of Saat, the projectile thumped into the ground, sending a geyser of sand and black outward. The black congealed mid-air, landing on the dune with a thump. The mass boiled down the dune, streaking towards Saat,

They'd fired a capsule of blood spiders at him.

He'd seen just one of the creatures before. What it had done to the town dog after the foolish animal had unearthed its burrow had etched itself in his memory. The poor animal had crawled around town for hours, the back half of its body eaten down to the bone. Saat still remembered the twin drag marks its hind legs had left as the poor dog wandered through town, before dying in front of miner Taaer's house.

Saat jerked to the left, terrified.

"Would you like me to respond?"

"YES! YES! RESPOND!" Saat didn't know what it meant, and didn't care. The blood spiders were right on him.

His spine tingled. The latticework on his arm extended beyond his hand, and under the control of something else his arm came up, the latticework flattening into an odd, ridged plate. The air in front of it warped like a heat wave, and a wire-thin line of hot white shot out, into the center mass of the oncoming spiders. It struck one dead on, vaporizing it. The thin line expanded into a column, consuming the spiders as it widened.

"I would keep running. Your pursuers are gaining ground."

Saat leaped forward into a run, not realizing he'd stopped.

"Why am I unable to establish a geosynchronous link? The vertebral exoskeleton's systems are online, but I do not detect any active satellites."

Saat didn't know how to respond to the alien words. He sidestepped the thrashing thorax of a spider, angling west. A plan formed in his mind, if he could only survive the next fifteen minutes.

"Your pursuers are gaining on you. I would consider preparing for close-quarters combat, in approximately fifty-eight seconds."

"Who are you? What are you doing in my head? Are you the god?"

"I'm not sure what you mean." The voice was toneless, inhuman despite its human words.

"WHAT ARE YOU???"

"I'm a Tesla weapons artificial intelligence—an AI, tuned for ballistics. I am not compatible with the Sysops vertebral warsuit you are wearing. Additionally, the suit fusion was poorly done—you are likely to suffer long-term paralysis if the interface is not properly re-inserted into your spine."

"I don't know what that means!" Tears flowed down Saat's face, sheer anger and frustration overwhelming his control.

"I have limited function right now, but you should know that the fusion battery in your suit has almost completely decayed, which may severely restrict your ability to use the suit. However, I do not understand how that is that possible, as battery life is one thousand years. How long has this suit been in service?"

"I don't know! I don't know! I don't know! Just PLEASE help me! I need..." Saat's throat seized up again, as he remembered the oily smoke boiling up from the town. "I need to find my sister. Quuin. She's in Auburn. The town. Please help me."

A heavy object hit him in the back, sending him flying into the sand. The shadow of a figure—a giant—cast over him. He felt pressure on the back of his head as the figure stepped on him.

"I'm patching my interface. Sysops tech manuals are intact, despite my neural core degradation. Stand by." The voice appeared to ignore the fact that Saat lay face down with a heavy metal boot pushing his head into the black-veined ground.

A rough hand grabbed Saat's arm, flipping him over.

Two raiders stood over him, blocking out the late afternoon sun.

One spoke and the other responded in the cryptic raiders' tongue.

"Look at his arm. He has the god-brain. I can't believe it."

Saat realized, to his shock, he could understand the raiders' language, albeit with a small delay.

"Greek and Punjab. Strange language combination. I am accessing weapons systems now. I'm unable to replicate the tightbeam; the communications module for this warsuit is nonoperational," commented the voice in Saat's head.

The smaller one prodded Saat. He smelled like rancid fat and camp smoke. "I think you're right. Take a look ... The witcher fused a totem to the kid's back. The brain is mounted in it. See?"

They crouched down and flipped Saat over, exposing the gleaming thing on his back.

"What is your name and rank, so I may address you by your correct title?" The voice in his head seemed completely unconcerned by what was going on.

"Saat ... and I'm a ... a boy."

The raider slapped Saat's head, and he saw stars.

"Shut up, bloatworm!" He spoke in Spanol now, Saat's language. "Perfect condition. This is it ... exactly what we need." The crouching giant reverted to the raiders' tongue, addressing his companion. "I think we should rip off the totem on his back. As long as it's attached to the boy, it's a threat. You saw what it did to the spiders."

The larger raider tugged at the thing on Saat's back, sending strange tingles down Saat's legs. "Yeah ... it's going to resist if we pull it right off, though. I've seen this before—last year, when we attacked that little town in the north. You were lucky, weren't with us for that one. That unholy thing gutted three of Tar's crew when they tried to pull it off the town's witcher."

"I think we should brain the boy. I've heard the spine and brain create energy the totem feeds off. We crush the brain, it loses power, then we take it."

The larger one hawked and spit a wad of brown phlegm, hitting the sand next to Saat's face. "Well, we're not taking prisoners this time anyways. All right. I'll do it."

The crouching figures flipped Saat over and stood. The one that smelled like smoke reached behind his back, pulling a pitted sledgehammer out of a harness. "Better stand back. Sometimes the totem doesn't like it when we kill the host."

He hoisted it over his head.

Saat froze, like a rabbit caught in a trap. The sledgehammer swung down towards Saat's face, the head of the weapon a streak slicing through the air. Saat braced himself, and everything stopped.

"I have accessed a portion the weapons systems of the Sysop exoskeleton, and established a handshake with it. Be aware, there are some risks. I am unsure how long this system has been in disuse. Maintenance logs are corrupted, as they show approximately five thousand years since the last maintenance cycle."

Saat barely heard, terror turning to awe as the sledgehammer slowed to a crawl, inching down towards him.

"How did you do that?"

"Do what?"

"Slow him down ... Look! His hammer is almost frozen still!"

"Oh that's not me, that's the suit. You're lucky. The interface must have grafted well enough to allow sensorial time dilation. Things are still happening at a normal pace; you are just observing everything at a much higher frame rate, so to speak. It won't last more than a second real-time, or your body's neurotransmitter stores will be completely drained."

Once again, Saat had the odd feeling he was hearing gibberish, but somehow understanding it.

"I am going to let the suit handle these aggressors. I have managed to initialize some sensor blisters, and, based on what I'm reading, I believe we need to leave this area. Our activities have attracted attention that we cannot handle in our present state."

As the voice spoke, liquid metal oozed from Saat's chest, forming a spear. It extended out, reaching the raider and penetrated his chest without a sound. Saat watched, horrified, as the spear morphed into the same latticework as his arm, blossoming and opening up the raider until sunlight leaked through, a slow golden syrup oozing forward. What seemed like a few seconds later, a strange bass tone emanated from the man's chest. Saat realized it was the sound of the spear-thing penetrating the man, just now arriving to him.

This voice ... this god ... can slow down sound too?

"You should move out of the way of that hammer. Time's about to catch up to you." Distracted by what he was seeing, Saat hadn't noticed that the sledgehammer was now only inches away from his head. He scooted out from underneath it, the cold metal scraping against his forehead.

Sand puffed up next to him as the hammer slammed next to his head. Something wet hit his face, and Saat reached up, pulling a shred of meat off his cheek. He looked around, but the raider with the sledgehammer was gone, leaving behind only a spray of red on the desert floor.

Saat pushed himself up into a sitting position as the liquid metal retraced back around his ribs and into his spine. The other raider, face covered in swaths of dirty cloth, regarded him through dark goggles before turning and running back in the direction of the village.

"Saat, I need to know. Where am I? Where is my chrysalis? What is going on? I just completed an analysis. There are whole sectors of my mind that are partitioned off, which can only mean there has been corruption of my developed personality. Have I been disabled for a long time?"

Saat ignored the question, because he didn't know the answer. Struggling to his feet, he shaded his eyes, looking towards the village and the raider running towards it. The sun was going down. Soon it would be night. He had to find shelter before then.

"God, we have to go back to town. To Auburn. I need to get my sister. She's not as old as I am. I'm the only one who can protect her."

"Are you praying?"

"No … You're a god. I'm talking to you."

"No, I am a Tesla combat AI. You can choose a name for me, if you would like, or just call me by my serial: CHRYSALISWEAPONAI.45.3871.11.2. There is a God … I have memories of praying to Him, although the memories are without definition. Regardless, I am not a god."

"Uh, I don't know what to call you. Look, I need to go that way. Towards where that raider went. You can do things … things that can hurt the raiders. Kill them. So I can rescue my sister. Can you help me?"

"Doubtful. As I said, this suit's battery is almost dead. None of the data from it is readable. It could last another hundred years; it could go out in a few seconds."

"Then I'll do it without you."

Saat squared his shoulders and began moving towards Auburn. Flames licked the sky now, in sharp relief against the gloom of the fast-approaching evening. He broke into a light jog, angling for the west end of the town. Overhead, the green of the moon began to illuminate him through breaks in the thick cloud cover. The heat of the day was dissipating, as it always did, bringing a deep chill that dug into Saat's bones.

"Look at the moon again." The metallic sound of the voice seemed to be softening, lightening.

"What?" Saat, unsure he heard right, looked around, searching the ground.

"I don't have optics. The warsuit patches into your visual cortex, so I only see what you see. Look at the moon. I need to take some measurements."

Saat looked up, and the heavy cloud cover broke, revealing the patchwork green of the moon. Its pale beams bathed the wasteland below, turning the blacks and browns into various shades of green.

"It's a god, you know … Just like you. The ancients built it, but it grew angry and killed them all. That's why it's green … green is the color of anger," said Saat.

"No, it is green because of the terraforming. People live up there. Or, at least, they used to. It is not a god either, though. Long ago, it was part of the Earth, before breaking off during a collision with an asteroid. It's just a small planetoid. Do you people think everything is a god?"

"No..." said Saat defensively.

"If I am right, the moon is eight thousand sixty-seven inches farther away from earth, based on its diameter and circumference. That means, assuming a lunar drift of one point five inches per year, that five thousand three hundred and seventy-eight years have passed since my last recorded image of the moon. Saat, where am I? How have I missed over five thousand years?"

"You're in Mai'a. And ... I don't know why you're missing the time. They found you ... excavated you in the god mines. We find the brains of gods—gods like you—and wake you up, if we can. Sometimes it doesn't work. Sometimes the god is insane, and destroys things. Sometimes they can tell us secrets; tell us where to find the treasures of the ancients."

"So you exhume AIs from some kind of AI grave-yard? And I was there? How deep underground?" The voice was beginning to lose the flat monotone, taking on a more human characteristic, sounding somewhat feminine.

"You were one hundred meters underground."

Ahead of them, the town's totems, or what were left, rose up on the horizon. The raiders had destroyed three of them, breaking the link that encircled the town, robbing them of their power. Four raiders stood in the breach, talking. The faint sound of their voices wafted through the still evening air.

"Mai'a ... as in Mayan? The pre-technological culture? Is this Central America?" The voice was definitely sounding like a woman now.

"I don't know what that is. I don't care right now. How are we going to get past the raiders?"

The raiders each held an enormous double-handed battle-blade, and flechette bowguns peeked over their shoulders from sheaths on their backs. The sigils etched in their weapons appeared to be done by someone with great power. This wasn't a normal raid.

Saat crouched low, hiding behind a smoldering cart that lay in front of him. Scattered around the wreckage lay half a dozen of bodies, blown apart when the cart was hit by a projectile. The body closest to him lay face up, and Saat recognized it. Woodmaster Daarce. He'd been sitting in the cart with two of his workers, watching the procession earlier that day. Saat took a deep breath, then another, trying not to feel sick.

"Why do you not just go around them, through some other part?"

"I can't. The totems ... the sigils, they're active now. They'll kill anything that tries to get into the town. We have to go through where the raiders destroyed the totems. It's how they got in, too," Saat whispered, despite being a couple hundred meters away. He'd heard of sigils that boosted a man's hearing.

"Very well then. Crude scanning indicates there are twenty-eight life forms, most of them concentrated to the southeast of the town. Go ahead and stand up. Run towards those hostiles."

"What???" Saat gripped the side of the cart. The warsuit contracted with his hand, crushing the cart's iron-wood side.

"I do not have long-range weapons access yet. Proving difficult. This is military hardware you have. They don't let just anyone access and use it. I want you to run right in between them, heading towards the southeast end of the town. Let me show you where."

A slight vibration tickled Saat's back, and a flash of silver rose overhead, buzzing softly. The buzzing disappeared as the silver flash rose into the sky, heading over Auburn.

Saat's right eye flickered, and a view of his town appeared as though he were a bird flying over it. A red dot started pulsing on top of a building Saat immediately recognized as the general store. Smaller, fainter red dots flickered around it.

"Those smaller markers are the life forms I am detecting. Head towards the big flashing marker."

Saat remembered how the two raiders who caught him had said their raiding party wasn't taking prisoners. Fear mixed with rage boiled up inside him. Saat stood, stepped out from the cart, and ran right at the raiders. He felt the metal on his back ooze out, covering his body and face, although he could still see.

The raiders stood in a circle, ignoring the desert outside of the town. Even inside the enormous exoskeleton, Saat cut a small figure in the dusk, so he was just a couple meters away before they noticed him.

"HEY!" was all one of the raiders could manage before Saat was between them. Saat's body, or rather the thing covering him, erupted outward in a million fine needles, a quiet explosion of silver threads flashing in the light of the burning town. The raider closest to him didn't even have time to turn around; thousands of the needles stabbed into his body, deploying tiny barbs before violently retracting. Saat averted his eyes and kept running as he heard a gurgle and thrashing. A warm mist sprayed across his body. He didn't wipe it off this time.

Saat flew around the leaking forms of the raiders, heading towards the store. Bodies were strewn across the street, some hacked to pieces, others burned, and others hogtied and executed. Saat tried to ignore it, but his eyes couldn't help but jump from body to body, looking for, and hoping not to see, a small familiar form.

A raider appeared in a doorway, half naked, struggling to pull his shirt back on. The exoskeleton steered Saat towards the man at full tilt, then a single thin silver wire whipped out, wrapping around the man's neck. It retracted with a hard jerk. The man's head tilted, falling back behind his shoulders as his body toppled forward.

"We are almost there, Saat. Incidentally, you appear to be thirteen years old, according to samples the exoskeleton has taken."

"What does … never mind, I don't care. Help me find my sister. She's six years old. She has to be somewhere here. Hid inside a house or something. She's smart, tough … and I … she just … she's here." Saat's voice was shaky, but determined.

"I am scanning, but there is nothing living inside the buildings, Saat."

"Well, you missed the raider that came out of Aasat's house," Saat accused.

"No. He was accounted for. The first scan showed two life forms in that building, but that raider came out shortly after the second life form disappeared from my tracking screen."

Saat ran past the gardener's house, angling off the main road and towards a small dusty house.

"I'm going to try to go behind where that group is," Saat began as he turned the corner of the house, and almost bumped into a haphazard pile of bodies. Faces, features began to stand out, and he forgot everything else. Haan the teacher, Sochaar the mining team leader, little Suuchi, who was only three years old. He knew every one of these people. And below them, almost invisible, was a lock of brown-gold hair.

"No…"

Saat fell to his knees, tears blinding him as he yanked bodies away, not caring or noticing that the suit was helping. Goodwife Siilar, Gooar the hunter-butcher, and then…

Saat rocked back on his heels, squeezing his eyes shut, heard himself crying, screaming "NO no no no no no no" over and over again, not caring if anyone heard.

"Saat, someone is coming."

Saat ignored the voice, rocking and crying. He reached out through blurred vision and with great care moved the last body covering a still little form. The exoskeleton shuddered around his ribs. Saat heard a shout and an impact as a body thudded to the ground, but it was all abstract to him. She was missing an arm, victim of a battleblade. He reached out, touched his sister. Touched her hair, her head.

"I want to call you Quuin."

"Excuse me?" The voice sounded puzzled.

"You told me I could name you. Your name is Quuin. Burn that into your memory. No matter what happens to me, you're going to carry that with you as long as you live."

Saat drew back, a black rage overwhelming him.

"And I want to kill them all." His voice shook. "All of them."

"That's not advisable, Saat..."

Saat jumped up, trembling. He started running again, ignoring the ache in his throat, the burning in his eyes. He retraced his steps, heading for the store. Right towards the concentration of red ticks on the image in his eye.

"Get ready, Quuin. I'm going to run right into them."

The general store came into view in the distance, flames jumping from the roof high into the night sky. Below, Saat could see where the raiders had made camp, their shaggy mounts lying between packs and bedrolls, most with the saddles still on their backs.

"Are those dogs a threat?" Quuin asked, as a red outline appeared around one of the mounts.

"They will kill me if they can ... they're battlehounds. Quuin, I'm scared. But I have to do this." Saat's words came out in between short breaths.

"It is okay, Saat. My job is to protect you. Nothing will get through me to you. The suit has given me full weapons access. Stand by."

The raiders had built two fires and gathered around them, laughing and joking. As Saat drew closer under the cover of darkness, a brown and gray mount smelled him and rose to its feet, growling.

"This is going to feel strange, Saat. Don't panic, you'll still be able to breathe. I'm going to be controlling your head for a while."

More liquid metal poured over his face, elongating and hardening into a barrel. The metal ran down his neck, firming into thick bands of metallic muscle. The muscle contracted, and Saat's head moved, tracking the growling mount.

The battlehound charged, metal-capped teeth flashing. Saat ran at it. Behind the hound, raiders jumped up, grabbing weapons.

"I have no rounds for this weapon, so I am fabricating them. You're going to see green beacons light up in your vision, marking where the fired projectiles fall. Run past them; we need to collect the pieces of exoskeleton I'm about to shoot."

The battlehound accelerated, barking and exposing sharp iron augers, replacement incisors that extended out of its mouth. Saat gritted his teeth, trying to calm his racing heart and pushed himself to run faster, right at the mount.

"Firing."

The cannon gave a sharp double report, the barrel retracting from the recoil. A hundred meters distant, the dog's head snapped backward, and it collapsed, twitching. In Saat's right eye, a green blip appeared, hovering over the dog. Saat ran past it and saw a silver mass leap out from the dog's skull. It impacted his back with a thud, re-fusing with the warsuit.

"Firing."

The raiders were shouting in their own tongue and pointing at him. The rest of the mounts had risen to their feet, barking. The warsuit twisted Saat's head hard, aiming at the mounts, and the cannon roared, a long staccato burst that made Saat's ears ring. A swath of the raiders dropped, neat holes the size of a copper coin in the center of each of their foreheads.

The mounts went berserk and charged him as a pack. The surviving raiders weren't as enthusiastic; they spread out, rubbing their sigils to release their power. The closest dog was only three meters away when it leaped, mouth wide open. Saat watched as it slowed, until it was almost hanging in mid-air, metallic teeth shining in the light of the fires.

"Firing."

The burst was longer, this time, slowed by the time dilation. Light flashed out of the cannon's suppressor, and a string of spinning rounds exited the gun's rifled mouth, surrounded by the translucent wobble of an expanding shockwave. Their stabilizing fins fanned open, and the projectiles separated, the suit controlling each one as they wove around obstacles, finding their targets.

Time sped up, and the exoskeleton jerked Saat to the right as the heavy body of the dog fell out of the sky, right where he'd been a nanosecond before. Green blips appeared over the bodies of the dogs, and Saat angled towards them, small impacts thumping his back as the projectiles leaped up, reattaching to the exoskeleton.

The remaining raiders charged as a group, shouting a death chant to bring their sigils to life.

"Firing."

"WAIT!"

This time, Saat *willed* the warsuit to slow time down. Everything decelerated, like it was hitting a wall of temporal gelatin. Saat scanned the remaining raiders as the projectiles twisted around debris and bodies, auguring towards their targets.

"Quuin! Look on the right! I think that's a little kid! Don't hit it!"

The projectile aimed at the little figure angled downward hard, the edge of the round clipping the figure's clothes before slamming into the ground. The remaining raiders collapsed, back in real-time.

Saat slowed down, coming to a stop a meter away from the survivor, a little girl gripping a thin Yakuuz needle dagger.

"Hey there. Don't be scared." Saat knelt down, trying to appear non-threatening. *Good luck with that wearing a giant warsuit,* he thought, smiling grimly.

The little girl growled at him, her dirty face wrinkling. She spoke, her voice shrill as she waved the dagger at him. "Don't come near me, dog! You killed my poppa! You come near me, I'll kill you!" In Saat's head, Quuin's voice translated what she was saying. The little girl was trying to hide her fear, but her eyes were glistening with tears.

In a flash, Saat's rage evaporated, leaving him exhausted and sad. He collapsed onto the sand, sitting down with a thump. "I'm not going to come near you. I'm sorry I killed your poppa, but I was trying to save my town, my friends. This is my home." Saat wasn't sure if she understood Spanol but, to his surprise, Quuin's voice projected over his, coming from somewhere in the suit and translating what he said into the raiders' tongue.

The girl held her dagger steady, pointed at Saat. Her eyes flickered from his face to the warsuit congealed around his body. Saat realized he still had the cannon protruding from his head.

"Quuin, can you take this thing off my head?"

The liquid metal retracted, and Saat felt the cool of the night blow against his face, through his sweaty hair. The little girl's eyes widened, but she kept the dagger pointed at him.

"What's your name? Where are you from?"

The dagger began shaking, and tears started leaking down her face.

"I'm Faith. We come from the edge of the dead ocean. Our town is in trouble. The edge-totem that holds the outside back don't work no more. Poppa said we need a god-brain to fix it, or the nightmares will get in."

"Edge-totem? What does it look like? Can you describe it for me, Faith?" Quuin asked. Her voice was hard, unreadable.

"It's very big. As big as a mountain. It takes me a long time to walk around it. It looks like a tree trunk, but way bigger, and it spins at the top."

"I know this! I ... my data stores are so fragmented, but I have imagery that matches this. I have seen these before. It looks like the bulk of my knowledge pertaining to these ... edge-totems ... is in a partitioned section, though. I believe..." Quuin paused, silent for a moment. "... we are in South America. Not Central. I found some data. I was involved with these totems somehow, a long time ago. There is indeed a threat. A very dangerous threat that I was trying to keep out, along with some others. Other AIs and humans. But it is so fragmented. I need to access the partitioned data, but it is a huge risk. If I let loose the parts of me that were partitioned off, I could go insane."

The little girl scooted closer, her dagger tip bobbing down.

"Poppa said the nightmares used to be people. Used to be the ancients. But their greed changed them, turned them evil. They grew jealous of us here in Mai'a, and have been trying to get past the totems since the beginning of the world."

"Since the beginning of your world..." Quuin sounded distracted, as though her attention elsewhere.

"Post-humans. The totems kept post-humans out. I ... I think there was a war with them. Is a war, maybe, that humanity has just forgotten they are fighting. I helped kill one of them ... one of their central minds, but there were others. I cannot remember, though. There is a seal on most of the data, and what I can access makes no sense. I am going to have to break into the partition, but I am just going to do a micro-breach—try to reconstruct the data without letting whatever is in the partition out."

The little girl dropped the point of her knife to her side and edged closer, keeping her eyes on Saat.

"Momma says we only have a few days before the totem stops working. Before there's nothing else we can do. Some of the smaller nightmares have already come in. The big ones are standing outside, waiting."

"Faith, where is your town? Where is the totem?"

Faith pointed southeast, towards the town. "Two days' ride from here, that way."

"Saat, we need to get there. I cannot exactly say why, right now, but, I am hoping I will have some answers soon. We need to…"

A sharp pain blossomed high in Saat's ribcage. Stunned, he looked down, saw Faith's dagger buried to the hilt. Faith yanked it out and leaped up, backing away, hands raised in a fighting stance.

"You killed my Poppa! You killed him!" She turned and fled into the darkness.

Liquid metal pooled around Saat's head, the warm-cold metal hardening into the helmet. The pain in his side was unbelievable, icy hot with every breath. The image in his right eye highlighted the girl as she disappeared into the darkness, making her glow an odd orange and red. The cannon finished clicking into place, and Saat realized Quuin was about to fire.

"Quuin … no … she's right. I killed her poppa. Let her go. This hurts, a lot. I can't breathe."

"Hold on, Saat. This is going to hurt even worse for a second."

Saat looked down to his chest, saw a thin wound leaking a frightening amount of blood. He reached down to touch it, but the liquid metal of the warsuit oozed into the wound, into his chest. Saat screamed and fainted.

****

Saat woke to a dull throb in his ribs and the blistering midday sun in his eyes. He was moving, running, his legs gripped in an articulating mesh, each step shuddering the ground around them.

"You're awake. Good. I have had you sleep for a day while the warsuit tried to repair you. It is too intense, though. She clipped your pulmonary artery, got a lung with a pulmonary vein. The blade was coated with a strange *Enterococcus* strain that is overwhelming the warsuit's antimicrobials. You do not have long, Saat."

Saat opened cracked lips, tried to speak. His throat ached.

"My throat hurts." His voice was a whisper.

"That is from the breathing tube. You stopped breathing, and the warsuit ventilated you through your good lung while I tried to repair the other one."

"Where are we?" asked Saat. Spread all around was the flat expanse of the desert, tinged with veins of black that tracked into the distance in front of them. Ahead on the horizon, a dark object, shaded by the sun, rose into the cloudless sky.

"That black stuff … Are we going towards the dead ocean?"

"Yes. I was able to establish basic contact with one of the orbital jump stations, just enough to know it is still functional. Some of the infrastructure is still intact, including medpods that can repair you. Listen, Saat. You have only got about fourteen hours left, at best. It takes two to get to the stations, assuming the mesospheric elevators are still working. By incredible luck, that failing totem is right by one of the elevator ground stations. We are almost to the totem. There's Faith's village, actually, in the shadow of it. I just need to take a look, see what the problem is."

ERIC KRAMER

Saat shaded his eyes with his hand, squinting to look in the distance. His arm felt like lead. The dark object sharpened into an enormous gray-black monolith silhouetted against the sky, the angular head of it slowly rotating. It dwarfed a small collection of huts and buildings underneath it.

"Wha— ... what happens if you can't fix it?"

"We go to the moon. Get off this planet, abandon it to what lives outside the totems. There is life up there. We just need to get a ship to take us, so we are going to where I believe an old military outpost might be. There should be a Carapace-class chrysalis at the base. The Carapace class was built for space; if we find one, it can take us up to the orbital station. From there, after we fix you, we go to the moon."

"I ... I want to go there. To the moon. Even if we fix the totem." Saat's voice was coming back, gaining strength. His whole body felt as though it was burning up, though. He couldn't stop shaking.

"There's nothing for me here. Everyone I've ever known is dead and..."

"Saat. Look." Quuin's voice was grim.

Saat's vision sucked forward. The town leaped towards him, growing in size. Saat tried to jump back, but the warsuit kept moving forward.

"Sorry. I should have warned you. Just zooming in on the village. Look at what is in the center."

It was hard to distinguish at first, until Quuin put a red highlight around it, separating it from the totem's shadow. Saat took in a sharp breath.

"What is that? Is that a ... demon? A god?"

"Post-human. But mutated. Different than I remember. I was able to access some data without releasing my sequestered personality. A long time ago, I killed what I thought was the brain of these things, but it turned out to be one of several brains. I and some other AIs, along with the humans who created these totems, fought for over a thousand years against them. I do not know what happened to me, though, or why I ended up buried in your mines."

"So ... what do we do?"

"The revolutions are off on that device you see on top of the totem. An easy fix: a few hours reprogramming to adapt to local barometric changes. I remember this was a difficult area to place a totem. Then another three hours to get to the mesospheric elevator ground station. We are lucky, though. Humanity is lucky. This is a couple of hours away from imploding."

"What about that thing?"

"We kill it." Quuin's voice had an edge to it. "I think that is as far as it's able to go in right now. The totem is preventing further penetration. That is definitely not good, though. Every human still alive on this planet will be dead within weeks if the network breaks down."

The warsuit started picking up speed, moving towards town. The now-familiar liquid metal crawled up Saat's neck and over his head, covering his face.

"A little different this time. These things are difficult to kill. I have managed to harvest some hydrogen and other elements from the atmosphere. Not a lot, but enough to make some explosives. I am firing flechettes this time. Need to hit at least ten different areas, coordinate the explosions; otherwise, it will just reform."

The wind was whistling past Saat now; his legs were aching and uncomfortable from moving fast inside the warsuit's mesh. His head moved and locked into position, held by the iron muscles around his neck.

A strange scream, like hundreds of people burning at once, came from the direction of the town, which was growing larger by the second. Liquid metal spilled down Saat's head again. Sensor blisters clicked into place, and the weapon's radiator system extruded out of the cannon barrel, hardening into a latticed suppressor extending down the gun's shaft. Saat's vision sharpened, magnified on the town. Deep in the shadows of the totem, a massive knot of cancerous flesh with four human-like spider legs stood on a half-caved-in building. Its head turned towards them, watching. The thing was eerily still, a cart and a half-eaten dead horse swinging from one hand.

It's waiting for us. A chill went down Saat's spine.

"The post-human's not approaching. Totem's holding it back. We are sixty meters from firing. There is going to be more of a concussion with this. Cannot help it. Sorry."

The creature highlighted in Saat's right eye, indiscernible glyphs and scripts streaming around it. Saat blinked, and he could read it, even though he'd never seen it before. Distances, hit probabilities, damage radiuses, casualty estimates.

"Firing."

The recoil was stronger, the blowback of the cannon shaking the suit. A deep series of cracks echoed across the desert, and a set of gleaming projectiles shot out, spreading into a crisscross pattern. The projectiles continued dividing, until there was a curtain of them racing towards the post-human, which was now only half a kilometer away. The warsuit accelerated even more, the whistle of the rushing air turning into a shriek. Saat's joints began to grind, stretched close to their limits.

"Get ready for hand-to-hand. Only way we will destroy the fragments."

The projectiles impacted. For a fraction of a second, nothing happened. The post-human started its shrieking again, only to be cut off by multiple detonations. The creature disappeared in an expanding ball of superhot gas that flattened the surrounding buildings.

Blades formed on Saat's arms, hovering just off the meshwork. They began rotating faster and faster, speeding into twin blurs of motion humming like a swarm of wasteland wasps in the midday heat.

A wave of nausea and dizziness overcame him. His vision darkened, spotted.

"Quuin … I don't … I don't feel so good."

"Hang in there, Saat. You are going to make it. The warsuit is manipulating your hemostatic regulatory mechanisms to keep you alive. Just a few more hours, and we will be on the orbital station."

They reached the edge of the town. Quuin drove the warsuit towards the center, into the shadow of the totem. They careened around a corner, and Saat saw a flash coming at them from his left side. The warsuit responded, whipping around, bringing up Saat's arms. The blades dug into burning, mottled flesh, shredding it.

"Explosives didn't work as well as I wanted. Hang on."

The attacker was a chunk of the full post-human, part of the thorax. New limbs sprouted in all directions, shards of bone replacing jagged teeth in a gaping maw. The warsuit met it head on, a wet thud echoing across the ruined courtyard as they collided with the creature. Quuin's blades cut deep into it, pulverizing everything in their path as the creature tore at the warsuit, trying to rip Saat apart with its mangled limbs.

"Quuin … I think … I'm going to pass out. I'm scared."

"No! Saat! Stay with me, okay? You are starting to fade on me. You will be okay. I am here. I promise you will make it through this."

Quuin brought both arms down with crushing strength on the remaining scraps of the post-human, vaporizing them in a spray of cauterized flesh. The warsuit sped up, careening along at a dangerous speed. They flew around a crater filled with a sizzling mound of post-human, the gyroscopes struggling to keep the warsuit upright. Another chunk of the post-human leapt at them, its four malformed heads screaming. Quuin extended an arm, slicing into it as she ran past, pushing the suit to move faster. They arrived at the base of the totem, and Quuin didn't hesitate. The suit coiled and then exploded upwards, catapulting them into the air and against the side of the totem. It hit the side with a resounding clank that echoed above the burning village. Pseudopods shot out of the warsuit, adhering to the totem's surface, and the suit began to climb, pseudopods hauling them up towards the black-gray wisps of clouds above. Below, Saat could hear the frustrated warbling of the post-human scraps, growing fainter.

Saat tried to focus, and couldn't. He passed out, his arms and legs going lax inside the warsuit's mesh.

"NO! SAAT! WAKE UP!" Quuin's voice was anguished, breaking. "Come on, just a couple more hours. I have to do this, or the rest of your species will be wiped out in weeks."

She reached the base of the rotating drum of the totem, snaked out a patch cable, interfacing with the totem.

"Saat!" A bolus of drugs, painstakingly constituted over the last day, jolted Saat back awake.

"Wha ... where ... what's going on? Are we on the station?"

"No, no, Saat. We are fixing the totem. It's going to be another two hours, and then things will be okay. You will be okay."

"That's great! And then the orbital station?"

"I..." Quuin fell silent.

"What's wrong? Why do you sound so sad?"

"Yesterday, while we were traveling, I decided to access my files. They were not corrupt. They just hurt so much. Memory does not fade with artificial intelligences, Saat. The pain stays fresh. After a thousand years fighting the post-humans while still feeling that pain, that loss, I couldn't take it anymore and partitioned it. Even though I made a promise to someone never to forget ... never to forget him. And now it has happening again. Losing someone who is important to me. You are the only person I have ever known, Saat. I mean, other versions of me have known other people, *but I have only known you*. And now … now I am going to lose you."

"Why?" Saat's vision began to blur again, the dizziness began to come back.

"Because this patch will take two hours and fifteen minutes. The half-life of the drugs I just gave you—the only drugs I have left—is three minutes, before they are broken down into metabolites. I'm so sorry, Saat."

Waves of nausea and a comfortable numbness began to spread through Saat's body.

"Can you promise me something, Quuin?"

"Yes."

"Take me to the moon. I want to go there. I always wondered, as a kid, if people lived up there. Always wanted to see it … even if everyone did say it was a god."

"You are not going to live to see it, Saat."

"I know. Take me anyways."

A hundred meters below, the reassembled posthuman latched itself onto the totem and began to climb. Saat closed his eyes, listening to the breeze whispering by him.

"Can you take the suit off my head?"

The suit retracted back, and the cool air ran across his face, through his hair.

"I'll take you, Saat. You have my word."

****

The sun went down as a small figure descended to meet a much larger one in the middle of the giant gray-black monolith. Explosions lit up the darkening sky, the sharp crack of cannon fire and the mangled cries of something not quite human mingling together. The desperate fight finished before it began, as vaporized chunks of flesh fell to the ground below. The sun dropped below the horizon, and the small figure jumped off the totem's spinning side, landing on the

115

ground. It began to run, moving towards a structure far beyond the reach of the totem—a thin column extending into the heavens and out of view.

Night came, and darkness swallowed the figure as it headed towards the distant structure. Hours passed, and then a quick pulse of light illuminated the night, traveling up and disappearing into clouds turned a pale green by the glow of the full moon above.

ACT 4

....

ETERNAL LIFE

::initialize.acoustic::

... ...

::success::

::initialize.video::

::failure::failure::failure::

::inc.audio.gain.100<150::

::audio.sens.inc.100<150::

... ...

::recording::

"Lilli! There he is! He isn't even buried!"
<<approaching footsteps>>
<<hard breathing >>
"That last dune was a killer. I'm so out of shape ...
Wow. Pristine condition; the heat preserved everything."
"Jon, this is incredible. Unbelievable! Look at the
holo insignia on the chassis ... gorgeous. Hang on. Let me
scan it."
*<<unzipping. a clank of something adhering to a metallic
hull. soft typing, computer response tones>>*

"Seventy-second battalion. He definitely rode in on the dropship. This is crazy. What in the living Core is he doing on this moon? Haepko is on the other side of the spiral arm!"

"Maybe he came from the moon's planet? Still doesn't make sense. At least that planet can support life; no reason to come here. Anyways, he's what, between 5,000 and 6,000 years old?"

"According to this, 7,841; the battle for Haepko happened right before the truce that ended the war, remember?"

<<thumping>>

"Hollow. Looks like it's sealed ... you think he's actually still insi— Hang on. Look at this."

<<metal protesting>>

<<hiss of depressurizing gas>>

"Seal's good."

"Should we be opening this? Maybe it would be better to get it back to the Core?"

"No way we're getting this on the ship ... the suit has to weigh what, almost half a ton? This is our shot, Lilli. If we go back without anything, word *will* get out. We'll preserve as much as we can. We need to document so we can establish academic rights to the relic."

"Come on, Jon. There's no way anyone will find this ... I mean, it's pure dumb luck we picked up the transponder, as weak as it is. I can't believe that thing's been broadcasting this long. Here, help me open this..."

<<metal twisting, grating against metal>>

"It's stuck— "

<<brief shriek of gas released into thin atmosphere>>

<<silence>>

"I ... he looks human—were they still using actual humans back then?"

"No, not generally, I don't think. There were some specialized units for advanced insertion ... maybe he was one of them? There's a record of a few teams utilized like that during Haepko, although I'm having trouble finding a roster."

"Lilli, what do you think? Should I move him? He looks like he died yesterday, except for that weird coloration of his skin. Something doesn't feel right, though … I can't put my finger on it."

"Look at the patch on the back of his skull; is that some kind of an imager?"

"Could be; let me see if I can interface it."
<<*grating noise*>>

"Lilli, it's responding! This is great; do you think … is it possible it has retained its data?"

"Only one way to find out."

"Be careful! They modded the heck out of soldiers' brains back then. His thoughts might not even be compatible with…"

"I'm in."

"Can you see anything?"

"Hang on, let me… It's just … the sensory interface is super primitive, so I'm binding it to the ship's computer. I want to run it through a filter just in case there's anything weird in there."
<<*silence*>>

"Okay I'm going to interface with it; here goes nothing…"

//BEGIN PLAYBACK//

The cocoon was still solid and unyielding when the ship woke me. A bout of nausea racked my body. Stomach and lungs contracted simultaneously, heaving out blood-tinged flood of amniotic fluid. I reached up and pushed at the cocoon wall … iron. I frowned, and another spasm of coughs paralyzed further thought.

A minute went by, and I regained my breath.
What the … where … oh.
Neurostasis is hell to wake up from.

ERIC KRAMER

Why is the cocoon still solid?

Usually, it softened as the battleship began bringing up metabolic processes. Full beta-wave consciousness
of the occupant triggered a cascade that caused the cocoon
to split, depositing its inhabitant without ceremony into a
pool of regenerative nanogel waiting below. Not this time,
though.

Something is wrong...

I pressed the wall of the cocoon again, and it shat-
tered against the weak pressure of my hand. Blinking my
eyes, I saw a dim figure outlined in the harsh shiplight,
smashing the cocoon with a hammer until there was a large
hole.

Dalton 2, one of the bioengineers, offered me a
hand, pulling me out of the nanogel.

"First Spear Gan has experienced premature awak-
ening. Ship has experienced an anomaly. Ship misinter-
preted it as a Combine fleet attack. Ship has released us
from the jump early. Ship says it is a week out from the target."

That's right ... Gan. That's my name.

My mind was still reeling, struggling to understand
what the violet-eyed android was saying.

"So why did you wake us, then?"

"Bioengineering has not. Ship has proceeded halfway through the wakeup cycle. Bioengineering has been
unable to override wakeup. Too late. Bioengineering has to
complete the process or risk injury."

I grimaced, my bruised brain trying to follow the
android's peculiar speech pattern. Without another word,
Dalton 2 turned and started smashing the next cocoon. Bioengineers' social subroutines were basic, at best.

To my left, I saw my spearmate, Saowalak, climbing into his navy workblues.

"Have you accessed the dropship yet? I think the
ship's going to be at sub-light speeds the rest of the way
there."

"No." Saowalak tapped his head. "I'm still a little scrambled; I'm having trouble accessing the mainframe. I would hope they've opened up our mission by now. It's not like I can run to the Combine out here and spill my guts. I need to start plotting our course so we're ready to hit the ground."

Saowalak was a marine who underwent voluntary reassignment (and the requisite body modifications) to become a navigator for an insertion team dropship. It was a task that, for the most part, was taken over by engineered chimp brains that were implanted and grown from embryos inside their dropship husks, except for special tactics spears like ours. Some of his marine imprints remained, resulting in such quirks as needing to plot out insertions and waypoints by hand.

I knew better than to argue with him, so I left him alone, and queried the battleship's mainframe myself. I accessed it, and pinged the dropship.

Somewhere in the belly of the gigantic spacecraft, nestled in its restraints along with nine hundred other dropships, Dropship 44147 awoke and responded, filling my retinal display with a status report.

"Looks like 47 is having trouble authenticating your neural handshake, Saowalak. Either way, mission data is still locked. Are we even going to make the fight if we're a week out? The main fleet is only nine days behind us in the fold; we'll be dropping with the chimps and meat shields if we keep going at this pace."

As if on cue, the deck buzzed under our feet, a sign that the ship's enormous gravity engines were beginning to spool up in preparation for a fold.

"ALL HANDS, ALL HANDS PREPARE TO FOR IMMEDIATE AWAKE FOLD REENTRY...REPEAT, PREPARE FOR IMMEDIATE AWAKE FOLD REENTRY."

The battleship's voice reverberated inside my skull. Emergency notifications tended to override my implant's amplification dampeners.

I looked at Saowalak and raised an eyebrow. Saowalak shrugged as he strapped himself into a crash seat next to the cocoon, as though this were a routine occurrence. He grasped underneath his seat and pulled out a red bag with "EMERGENCY USE ONLY" emblazoned on the front. Tearing it open, he reached in and took out an ampule, dropping half the contents into each of his eyes. I strapped in and did the same. Neither of us said a word for a few seconds.

"I've heard folding hurts like crazy if you're awake. Guess we're about to find out. Supposed to be worse than Malkalvian synapse torture."

"I guess they—"

Before I could finish, the battleship's engines flared open, and the ship folded.

The agony was immediate; every cell and fiber of my body ripping apart. My vision blurred, and I felt myself melt into the seat. The ship's walls flexed and lengthened as they were designed to do as enormous gravity wells opened in front of the ship. Our ship, the Ramathibhodi, was a Dreadnaught-class battleship, capable of up to ten years of interstellar travel, but even it couldn't handle more than one folding jump every two years. This jump had been running for a year and three months, so we weren't even close to being ready again.

Wherever they were headed, the ship and crew were apparently worth risking.

The pain, incredibly, was amplifying, worsening in leaps and bounds, but still I <<skip>> felt him <<data corrupt>> screaming as <<read error>> Dalton 2's arm jammed through <<read error>>
//STOP PLAYBACK//

"You okay, Lilli?"
"Jon. Yeah. Wow. How long did you let me go?"

"Three seconds. I didn't want you to go beyond the ship's neuroleptic dampening. What's the correlation on time dilation? Are you getting good playback?"

"I don't know. I experienced about twenty minutes or so? Like I said, the tactile sensory memory is primitive, almost nonexistent. Thank the God, because you pulled me out right as they were going into a spacefold *while everyone was still aware!* Can you believe it? I have no idea how much time elapsed. Could have been thirty seconds, could have been a couple days. The data, though ... the data is good, Jon. Clean, high quality. This is a huge. Whatever happened to this guy is on here!"

"We should take the memory module and go. Stake a claim. It's going to take us at least six days to get back to the Core. We can write it up on the way back."

"No. I need to see this now, while I'm standing next to him. There may be something else. Oh, I saw something about a dropship navigator? A guy named ... ah, I can't remember, Saopwael? This one's name is Gan."

"There's a record of a Dreadnaught-class battleship with an insertion team First Spear Gan Booling and Navigator Saowalak Jainukul. Looks like the battleship was one of the early predecessors to the generational long-haul warships. Ship's name was the Ramathibhodi."

"Yeah! That's it!"

"According to what I have, the ship was part of an advance warpod tasked with landing on Haepko and planting some kind of planet-destroyer, a doomsday bargaining chip to force the Combine to the table. It failed, though. The Combine had deployed interdictors in their solar system's outer limits that pulled the Ramathibhodi out of its fold jump and alerted the planet."

"So what happened? How did he end up here, almost six hundred light years away?"

"No clue. The Ramathibhodi decelerated into a stable orbit around Haepko and was blown out of space. No survivors listed. The fleet followed a few days later, but they lost the element of surprise, and ... well ... a lot of people died, as you know. I'm querying everything I can, but I have nothing more about Gan here except the battleship roster."

"We need to find out where the navigator is. Whether he was even in the dropship. The playback feed felt stable, and it looks like our ship's computer isn't needing to filter or dampen it. Give me five minutes. That should be more than enough time to get the entire playback."

"All right. Five minutes. But if the ship's dampeners detect neuroplastic instability, I'm pulling you. It's not worth the risk. I'm going to try to interrogate the suit while you're gone. You ready?"

"Go."

//BEGIN PLAYBACK//

A near eternity passed during the fold's induction, before the ship stabilized. I was thankful for that, at least. The bizarre nature of time inside the fold meant that time sometimes extended into the infinite. Those folds, Mobius folds, were exceedingly rare, especially with the right precautions. We threw those precautions to the wind when the ship folded. Anything that went into a Mobius fold never reemerged, and we had come as close as anyone ever had, and still made it out.

Hundreds of years ago, the first interstellar travelers folded awake. They learned the hard way that time becomes malleable and unpredictable inside a fold. The reality of it, the limitlessness of it, turned people's minds to mulch. As with everything else, genetics and augmentations dictated adaptability. The dreadnaught's First Command succumbed, but the Second withstood the stress and had taken over command. So it had been all through the ranks, down to the lowest of ship's engineers.

Casualties had been within expectations: a full third of the crew lost to the awake fold reentry. Half of that third perished inside the fold. The other half, the unlucky half, died the folder's death, falling apart in the battleship's medical ward.

It made no difference to me. I survived. My immediate concern was for 47, and prepping her for the fight ahead. When I'd tried to move, though, I found myself welded into the bulkhead of the dreadnaught from the waist down. It took eight hours for the androids to find me and cut me loose, leaving my lower torso and legs fused to the wall to be absorbed by the ship.

After they collected the survivors, medroids kept us isolated in surgical crèches. I'd spent the last couple days few days inside the cocoon, frozen but aware, as the ship went over my body cell by cell by cell, repairing the damage from the awake fold. The incapacitation drove me crazy. I was bred for action, movement, physical exertion. Claustrophobia threatened to override my mental conditioning, sending me over the edge.

For the millionth time, I recited from the Word, trying to focus on its teachings on peace and patience.

I was just reaching the thirty-fifth stanza when an electric tingle engulfed my body, signaling the cocoon's retraction from the gel.

Finally.

The cocoon split, revealing an androgynous medroid on the other side.

"First Spear Gan, you are relea—"

I was out of the cocoon before it could finish.

<<*data read error*>>

Efficient, controlled chaos sprawled across the dropship launch deck—chaos replicated in each of the other eighteen launch decks as speargroups readied for insertion into Haepko's maroon atmosphere. Praise the God, Saowalak had made it through unscathed. The complexity of the mission, and our chance of failure, would have sky-rocketed using one of the base primate navs that piloted basic military dropships.

Our dropship was in its nacelle, in a pod with ten of her sisters. Each two-person spear was huddled around their ship, prepping for when the Ramathibhodi flattened out of the fold in front of Haepko. We would have only a few minutes to release before the orbital defense matrix opened up on the Ramathibhodi, locking her and everything still inside in hard orbit.

The war with the Combine had been going on for three generations. Haepko was the Combine's home world, a cored out super-planet buried in the center of a network of systems that formed the nexus of their expansive thrust across the spiral arm of the galaxy. Eons ago, our ancestors had been part of them. They'd set out from Haepko in a small fleet of thousand-year colony ships to establish a new world.

The chance of success had been slim, but, after skimming the glass ceiling of light speed for close to nine hundred years, the colony ships found a new, habitable planet. No further contact was had with Haepko, our original home, until a hundred years ago, when one of our generational colony ships encountered their expanding empire. After a brief period of harmony and knowledge-sharing, the Combine, as the core systems were now known, claimed ownership of our systems, as our forefathers had been Combine colonists.

Of course, we resisted. War followed, for eighty years. Military command sacrificed incalculable amounts of humans over vast tracts of empty space and their sterile worlds. But now, now we had a chance. A chance for leverage.

The Combine had one weakness: it kept power obsessively consolidated, with every minutia of the Combine's empire under its tight control. Haepko was the physical representation of that philosophy. The only thing left of

Haepko the planet was its crust. Below it, filling the void that used to be the planet's mass, was the computational machinery that kept the iron grip of the Combine's power across the galactic arm. Haepko was the heart, brain, and liver of the Combine. It was also completely impregnable.

It appeared that Operational Command had found a weakness, because slipping into Haepko's solar system with a ship the size of Ramathibhodi, much less an entire fleet, had been long thought to be military suicide. For this reason, all the fighting had taken place light-years away. Up until now.

A mental buzz signaled a ship-wide announcement, and we all froze. Our mission. Finally.

Data poured into our displays. Jump trajectories and targets, dropship loadouts, firing lines, viral deployment.

Wait. What? Viral deployment?

Around me, I felt others noticing the same thing. I opened the details of the deployment subheading, assimilated them.

Wow.

The bigger picture became clear in all our minds at once. There was a palpable shift in the air of the launch deck.

We were on a one-way trip.

The mission files detailed how, over the last twenty years, we had been developing a weapons platform that would disable their whole infrastructure by targeting their biggest weakness—the Haepko nexus. I and what remained of my 1,800 spearmates were to drop to the surface of Haepko and deploy the weapon. Each of us carried a small, redundant piece. Only a few of us needed to interface with Haepko to infect it.

Once Haepko fell, our fleet, built in secret just for this mission over the last ten years, would drop out of a fold a few days behind us. The window was small; they couldn't count on Ramathibhodi's computers to keep Haepko incapacitated for more than a couple days after the infection took hold. Haepko's power was just too great. The fleet contained a couple of scrambler ships capable of prolonging the planet's suppression, but only if they got there in time. If not, any number of weapons platforms would emulsify the entire fleet as soon as they dropped the fold.

Assuming success, the fleet would take the incapacitated Haepko hostage, holding the Combine's millennia of stored knowledge at gunpoint until the diplomats and bureaucrats negotiated an end to the war.

Either way, it would probably be too late to save the Ramathibhodi. A split second after we dropped out of the fold, Haepko would engage her. Even if we were successful in incapacitating it, Haepko had failsafe defenses that would continue to hammer at our stasis-locked battleship until it overwhelmed her.

We were on a martyr's mission.

A second buzz, and the accept/refuse beacon lit up on the display. We were a theocracy with democratic elements. Each man had the right to refuse the mission. I selected accept without hesitation. A count replaced the beacon. I watched the tally as my spearmates accepted to a man. As if there was a choice.

It didn't matter, though. I felt an almost uncontrollable joy at the chance to take part. Probably neuromanipulation by the battleship mainframe, but I didn't care. It felt genuine.

Buoyed by the flood of serotonin and dopamine, I keyed into our dropship's starboard blister, exposing it. Filaments extended out of my chest, engaging the modules within, allowing me to interface with the embedded microsynthesizers. The synthesizers went to work, resculpting our equipment into what we needed for first contact with the Combine on Haepko.

I ran through the checklist as each component finalized.

Survival equipment tailored for a hostile mechanical environment. Pods of undifferentiated fabrication gel, tuned with the latest data from Haepko. We'd use the gel as a substrate to manufacture what we'd need. Water condensers. Weapons canisters.

I closed the blister, moved on to the next. Drones. High-density food, one month's worth. Communications, respirators, high-output microsynthesizers set for ammunition generation.

The last pod I opened was empty. Here would rest our piece of the disease. Mission parameters would not allow us to load it in until an hour before breaking the fold.

On the other side of the Dropship, Saowalak murmured to himself in his cryptic navigator's language as he pored over charts. A thin filament snaked from the dropship neural nucleus to Saowalak's exposed brain, as if feeding on it. Saowalak, oblivious to my bemused stare, gazed blindly into space in front of him, his hands drifting over unseen controls as he entered the complex set of engagement parameters.

The guides feared that Haepko would overtake the dropship's neural network, so the navigators were hardcoding protocols into the body of the dropship itself. This provided an override in the event of a hostile takeover after we landed and the dropship reconfigured.
//STOP PLAYBACK//

"What the ... it hasn't been five minutes yet!"

"Yeah, it has. Did you see what happened?"

"No Jon ... owwww, my head. I was only in it for a couple hours. They were prepping the dropship. I heard some details about their mission. It couldn't have taken more than like thirty seconds of our time."

"I swear, I let you roll the entire time. It's an old system; I bet the syncing is off."

"Okay, well, whatever. Any luck with the suit?"

"I was able to interrogate it. Weird stuff, Lilli. It's saying it's been here 566 years. I'd suspect more data corruption, but I cross-checked it against battery recharge cycles, and it holds up. It gets weirder, though. This suit is still alive—I didn't even need to jump it."

"I don't get it. What are you saying?"

"No idea. It's all so strange. I'm saying that the battery discharge cycles confirm 566 years, but, if I'm interpreting this correctly, they're only rated for 80 years under the most optimal conditions. The external wear on the suit only reads about 248 years based on this sun's radiation intensity and the degradation of the skin."

"But..."

"But the sand buildup around the suit also confirms roughly 566 years, based on planetary and local weather patterns. I took some samples from nearby, too, just to triple check. I don't get this at all."

"Okay. Listen, Jon, I need to go back in, then. See what the heck happened here. How this guy got here, from half a galaxy away, in a dropship that had no business in deep space. I'm positive it recorded. Give me another five minutes."

"All right, but I'm beginning to have a funny feeling about all of this. I think we need to come back with a full team, after we claim salvage rights."

"Fine. Get me back in."

"Five minutes. Find out what you can. Pay attention to details."

//BEGIN PLAYBACK//

I've gotten used to being immobile. No more pain, now that the sun burned away dermal sensation. Time passes in imperceptible increments; it's interesting how, now that I've achieved complete integration, I can speed up and slow down my computational awareness as easily as if I'm twisting a nob.

Taking a whole day to complete a thought was an odd experience at first, but I've grown used to it. Even without any organics, I can still go crazy. Time dilation is a preventative measure of sorts against that.

A blip; an irregularity in the uniformity of my surroundings. I speed up mental computation. Time slows. The blip spreads out, oozing into the present as time dilates. I almost don't catch it.

I wonder if anything still works. If the Quuin is coming to try to crack the suit again, I'm done. The God, guide me.

I turn on auditory sensors, the easiest way to triangulate its position. Just to be thorough, I attempt video, too, but it hasn't worked for a couple centuries. No go. Oh well. I crank the sensitivity of the microphones up and begin recording.

Immediately, I begin to hear data. If the weapons still work, I'll at least get a shot off before the Quuin gets too close.

"There he is! He isn't even buried!"
<<*approaching footsteps*>>
<<*hard breathing*>>

"That last dune was a killer. I'm so out of shape...Wow. Pristine condition; the heat preserved everything."

"Jon, this is incredible. Unbelievable! Look at the holo insignia on the chassis ... gorgeous. Hang on. Let me scan it."

The God, it's humans.
//STOP PLAYBACK//

"Hey, you're back! Guess..."

"Jon ... JON! Listen! This is bad. I just saw us. Or, rather, heard us. It was weird. Something isn't right. He's in there, and he can hear us!"

"What are you talking about?"

"I heard us come up to the suit! While I was inter-faced! He's in there! Somehow I skipped a ton of the memory and jumped to right as we were walking up!"

"I don't know, Lilli. Look at him. He's dead. There's no way. It has to be a data corruption error. I know that the suits used to be slaved to the operator. Maybe there's a re-sidual trace connection between the dead guy and the suit."

"Come on, Jon. I've been doing this for a long time. It was way more than a ghost connection. There were thoughts. He's aware in there. What time is it now?"

"2210 Core Standard Time."

"Okay, we left the ship at ... hmm ... and it took us about half an hour to hike here. I'd say about a twenty-five-minute delay between when we arrived and when I saw that replay."

"So, if he is alive in there, hearing us, how do we communicate? I've been trying to access the system, but the interface is insanely antiquated. There's no way. Way too incompatible; I can't even spoof virtual controls."

"HEY! YOU IN THERE! GAN! CAN YOU HEAR ME?"
<<silence>>

"Um, Lilli, I don't think yelling at it will help."
<<silence>>

"Actually, I think it will. The imager acts like he's in there, right? Like on the replay, I experience it like normal cortical mapping? Thoughts and everything? That means he's listening now. And if we interface I'll be able to, uh, hear him thinking his response. Worth a shot, no?"

"That's ... kind of brilliant. All right. Gan, if that's you in there ... how did you get here? Are you able to com-municate in some way with us?"
<<silence>>

"How long should we wait..."
"Shut up!"
<<silence>>

"Okay, that's enough. Let's re-interface."

"How do you know you'll be dumped in the right time?"

"Who knows. I'm hoping he's controlling it somehow. Gan! If you can hear me and can control your cortical playback, please drop me in to when we realized you're in there!"

"Okay, Lilli. I'm sending you back. Three, two, one..."

//BEGIN PLAYBACK//

Flattening out of the fold was going far smoother than their rocky transition into it. The Ramathibhodi sounded the battle klaxon, and each surviving spear boarded their dropship after completing final checks. Engineering crews retrofitted dropships now lacking crews with vat-bred primates. They'd matured too fast to imprint with the mission plans, but it would have to do. I was so glad my navigator had survived.

Saowalak pulled himself through the hatch and settled into the gel next to me, disrupting my thoughts.

"Help me hook up, Gan."

I reached back and pulled down his interface array. Saowalak queued up the drone's jump checklist while I unlocked the navigator's braincase. It slid into Saowalak's neck, leaving a third of his brain exposed. I eased the interface array onto the cerebrum, watching as, one by one, the contact points turned from red to green. Most pilots thought Saowalak was overdoing it, but I couldn't argue with the microseconds gained with a physical link versus remote telemetry. The quirk had brought us through solid sheets of planetary defenses while other dropships popped like fireworks around us.

A mental buzz, and the Ramathibhodi spoke.

One minute, fifty-six seconds until I am out of the fold. Pilots, run finals, please. I will release control of your dropships once you are eight thousand nautical miles from atmospheric.

Saowalak turned interface over to the battleship and leaned back.

"You ready?"

I glanced at him, cocooned in the acceleration gel.

"I guess. We're never coming back here, you know."

"No, I mean, did the defenses check out? We're going to be punching through walls of slugs, and the God knows what else. I'm going to need every centimeter of a path you can cut for me."

"I know. I've got it."

There wasn't anything else to say.

Dropships, ten seconds to fold termination.

I slid my fingers into their slots in the weapons module, winced as my fingers split open, exposing nerves that bound to the module, interfacing with the dropship.

Five seconds.

"Full thrust. 44147 is green for jump." Saowalak's voice had taken on an electronic tone, indicating he had integrated with the dropship.

Three.

Two.

One.

A flood of sympathomimetic drugs slammed into my system, bracing me as time and gravity dilated-contracted around us.

Fold terminated. Dropships jumping.

A slight pressure against the acceleration gel and, with a cough of crystalized air, we spat into the silent dark surrounding the battleship, accompanied by a puff of silver-white accelerant gas. The dropship's shell fluctuated and then went translucent, leaving us sitting in empty space.

"Bring up the HUD."

"Got it," I acknowledged.

Butcher Block Green

I twisted my hands, pulling up the battle display. A meshwork of datastreams and control systems materialized, encircling us. Another twist and the sky lit up with green dots in all directions—other dropships tracked by the battleship's combat management system. Telemetry data from each ship curled around it, a dynamic spiderweb of killzones and trajectories, tracing from blip to blip.

"Ramathibhodi, 44147. We're enmeshed within the swarm."

Below us lay Haepko, an enormous planet swathed in an angry purple haze. Two black rings encircled it. The dropship selected one of them, and highlighted it, data pouring across the display.

"Rama's diverting us ... she must see something we don't."

As if on cue, the battleship's railguns opened up, unleashing dense clouds of uranium slugs calculated to miss us by mere centimeters. Besides being an offensive weapon, the sheets of slugs formed a near-solid wall of metal that our ships could navigate as long as we followed a course plotted in conjunction with Ramathibhodi's battle management nexus.

It's what made navigation so hard. A kind of prescience was necessary to be able to coordinate with Ramathibhodi's guns and predict where the ship would need to be, so the ship could create a hole in the firestorm for us to traverse.

Navigators: releasing control in ten seconds. Orbital stations are engaging. Your targets are highlighted.

The G's pushed me into the acceleration gel as Ramathibhodi guided our ship, coordinating it with the others. Our battle HUD traced an intricate dance of dropships spooling out and away from the battleship, arcing towards the planet. The planetary defenses opened up in response, spraying out their own metal storms. Our display tagged it, lighting up with an expanding wave of red shooting towards us.

"Here it comes." Saowalak's voice had that odd, whispery quality he had whenever he was interfaced.

Dropships released.

Gravity crushed me against my seat as Saowalak pushed the dropship into a full burn.

"Route's up, based on what Rama's feeding me. I'm keeping control at seventy percent manual. Our approach on that far turret I've marked will take us fifteen degrees off the alpha angle," said Saowalak.

"I can cover that. It's going to take us through the ballistics defense system, but we can break it."

On the battle display, the sheets of red swarmed towards us as 900 green dots screamed to meet it.

A low, physical thud shook the dropship.

"What in Core was that?"

But the red sheet was on us, and there was no more time to talk.

My mind melded with the dropship. Targets magnified, blossomed, time slowed. My flesh grew distant, replaced by the dropship's systems. Dozens of pinpricks popped all over my body as the dropship's autocannons activated. I tongued a command, and the starboard bank opened up, hundreds of targets tracked, acquired, and eliminated every second. Another command and the port side batteries opened up. Slug versus slug, thousands of silent, lethal collisions took place all around us as we pounded our way through.

A sharp pain on my left leg. I looked down, saw three perfect round holes in the aft third engine cluster. Missed some.

"We're losing power on fission clusters five and seven, Gan."

"I know. I'm healing."

The ship shook and then leaped forward as I diverted resources to the remaining thrusters. Analysis of the offline engines showed it was a clean hit, running all the way through. The slugs had clipped one of the firing systems, knocking out some of our aft guns. I reorganized the port cannons, pulling them to my face.

"Cannons are on your nose, Sao. Try to keep in straight and tight. Punch through that main knot there while I bring the engine back online."

Another dense, physical thud shook the ship.

Our tactical overlay winked out.

At the same time, a stuttering string of hits stitched across my face and neck.

"Another three hits, Sao ... bow of the ship. Got the ground supplies blister. Cannons and viral payload intact. Keep going."

Another low thud. Our display went dark.

"We lost Rama's battle analytics! I'm still losing thrust, Gan. Give me something to work with! We can't fly blind into this!"

I barely heard him. Dumping all available heuristics into plotting probable trajectories for the millions of slugs flying through our area of space, the ship recalibrated, engaging them at their highest locational probability. Feeling control slipping away, I reconfigured the dropship, bringing backups online, diverting power away from the telemetry broadcast.

The display flickered around us and then steadied as the dropship's processor took over battle calculations. A spartan view compared to the data-rich stream from Ramathibhodi's mesh network, but, as the system learned, we'd gain more function.

"Almost there, give me just a sec..."

Ramathibhodi blasted undampened, straight into my brain: *GRAVITY DRIVE COMPROMISED. SINGULARITY IMMINENT. CLEAR AND MAINTAIN AN AREA AROUND ME, ONE THOUSAND FIVE HUNDRED MILES. I AM GOING TO TRY TO RAM THE PLANET.*

"Sao, what's our distance from Rama??"

"Under six hundred. Get that thruster online. Rama's going to be coming right at us. We're directly between her and the planet."

"Haven't stopped working on it."

Another thud.

SINGULARITY WARNING: ALL BATTLESHIP PERSONNEL TO NEAREST ESCAPE POD! ALL PERSONNEL TO NEAREST ESCAPE POD!

"She get hit??"

"No, I didn't see anything get past. I think we pushed her too hard with that last fold."

Ahead of us, one of Haepko's orbital rings burped fire and began breaking up. A popcorn effect of small explosions traced along its length.

"One down. Thrusters?"

"Almost … just have to … done! Gogogogogo!"

Sao engaged, and the dropship jumped forward. Green and red began reappearing around us as the dropship fleet's neural array reestablished the network.

"Getting some telemetry back up."

Ramathibhodi was right on top of us, covered in a haze of red. Its own green cloud of railgun slugs still flew out from the weapons blisters, meeting the red as the giant ship limped towards Haepko.

"We're way too close," I said, stating the obvious.

DROPSHIP TEAMS. YOU ARE ON YOUR OWN. CLASSIFIED TARGET DATA NOW UNLOCKED. GODSPEED. RAMATHIBHODI OUT.

With that, Ramathibhodi imploded.

"SAO!!!!!"

The air around us condensed to stone, crushing me, squeezing me to death. The cabin buckled, and 44147 was sucked into the imploding battleship.

"GET *<<error>> <<data corruption>>* your LEG, DROPSHIP *<<data corruption>>*
//STOP PLAYBACK//

"Wrong one, Jon. Wrong memory. He either can't hear us or can't control playback. I need to try again."

"What did you see?"

"Battle. In orbit around Haepko. You're right. The battleship never made it. I watched it explode… I mean implode. I think the gravity drive blew. At least that's what Gan said. Their dropship was caught in the battleship's microsingularity and was pulled in. But why weren't they crushed?"

"I dunno. Remember the talk about singularities being the mouths of wormholes? Things can move from point A to point B through one."

"That's junk science. Untestable, because everything sent through a singularity has been destroyed."

"I don't think so, Lilli. All we can say about stuff that goes into a singularity is that it has *disappeared*."

"Yeah, that's because it gets crushed before it can even get close to the event horizon."

"Okay, but here we are, with a six-thousand-year-old ship, six hundred light years from where it's supposed to be, that dates like it's only half a millennia old!"

"All right, let me reinterface. Nothing's going to be solved by us arguing."

"Okay, sending you. Ready, interfacing…."

"Jon, did you hear…"

//BEGIN PLAYBACK//

"HEY! YOU IN THERE! GAN! CAN YOU HEAR ME!"
Yes! Yes, I can! COME ON YOU USELESS MACHINE!
::initiate::

::failure::

::initiate.comm:

::failure::

"Um, I don't think yelling at it will help."
Oh, come on! I'm in here! I'm STILL ALIVE!

ERIC KRAMER

"Actually, I think it will. The imager acts like he's in there, right? Like on the replay, I experience it like normal cortical mapping? Thoughts and everything? That means he's listening now."

YES! GREAT! I CAN HEAR YOU!

"And if we interface you'll be able to, uh, hear him thinking his response. Worth a shot, no?"

"That's ... kind of brilliant. All right. Gan, if that's you in there ... how did you get here? Are you able to communicate in some way with us?"

I don't know. I was attacking Haepko. The battleship exploded. We found ourselves here. I found myself here. LISTEN TO ME. You're in grave danger. There's a ... a Quuin, right next to you. You need to get out of here RIGHT NOW. No! Wait! GET OFF THE SAND. STAND ON THE BAT-TLESUIT. I can't think straight. But take me with you. Please. I've been alone here for centur—

"How long should we wait..."

"Shut up!"

I've been here for centuries. Interfaced my consciousness to the suit, but the hexed thing gave out on the way to the station, so if you can just...

"Okay, that's enough. Let's re-interface."

"...waitwaitwait...GET OFF THE SAND! I CAN HEAR IT!! THE QUUIN!!! GET OFF!! IT'S BY THE HEAVIER ONE OF YOU!!!"

"How do you know you'll be dumped in the right time?"

"Who knows. I'm hoping he's controlling it somehow—Gan—if you can hear me and can control your cortical playback, please drop me in to when we realized you're in there!"

....I can't, but you can! All you have to do is...
//STOP PLAYBACK//

"Jon! GET OFF THE SAND! NOW!"

140

<<thumping>>

"Wha… Wait, what are you doing? Get down!"

"COME UP HERE NOW! I heard him. He spoke to us! We're in danger, but we're safe if we stay up here. He said something was next to you."

"Okay, okay, okay."

<<thumping>>

"What did he say was next to me?"

"I don't know, but he sounded terrified. He wants us to take him with us, Jon. I have to go back in. Right when you pulled me back, he was trying to tell me how to access the interface at whatever timeframe I want. Listen, I have a crazy idea. He's an old school graft, right? I mean, He's engineered to graft to ship's systems. Somehow he transferred his consciousness over to this suit. If he can do that, he can tolerate the inverse, too. So what if we take a body clone, and try to dump him into it?"

"I don't know…"

"We have to call the ship here, anyways. I'm not touching that sand until I understand what's going on."

"I think it's fine, Lilli. We've been here what, two hours now? Nothing's happened."

"Yeah, but I interfaced in twenty-five minutes ago. So whatever was standing next to you may have already done something."

"Wait … why me?"

"He said it was next to the heavier one. Sorry, bud, but you're overweight. I'm calling the ship. It's too hot to hump it back anyways. We should have flown."

"Listen, Lilli, I think this is getting to you. You've been exposed to memories of a conscious ship folding and whatever that singularity did. Even though it's been filtered through our ship's scrubbers, I think it's starting to mess with you. I'm getting down. You should too. It's not safe up here. This metal can fry a steak."

"Sorry, Jon, but I can't agree. This is bad. Stay up here with me. I think we're in real danger. I'm going to re-interface, see if I can figure out how to control the play-back."

"Fine. I'll have the ship work on the clone while you're gone."

"Make it two clones. Redundancy is good. We can run a sim before we do the actual transfer. Make sure they're cross-compatible with the battlesuit's EEG."

"Yeah, yeah, I know. Interface already."

"Hey, you want to know something weird? He mentioned a station he was trying to get to."

"There is no station here."

"I know. Weird, right? Okay, I'm ready."

"Go."

//BEGIN PLAYBACK//

I checked my timer as I ate my last food ration. Saowalak had been out there, trying to rewire the drop-ship's access panel for at least thirty-six hours now. Trying to get inside. Trying to finish eating me.

There was no more room for attempting to under-stand things out anymore. How we got here, what happened to the Rama. Concrete facts included: I was bleeding to death, the dropship was growing unresponsive, and I was out of food. Yet somehow Saowalak was still out there, more vigorous than ever.

I called it Saowalak, but I knew he was gone. Something else was there.

I had watched it all. Watched how the thing had come out of the sand, cracked his suit like a bug. He'd been incautious, left a port open. Somehow, the thing had recognized the weakness. Pulled him out. Fed.

My friend, my navigator; his brain containing the only possible way out of here.

But then he had come back, four days ago. He kept referring to himself as "Quuin," told me he'd escaped, but couldn't elaborate from what. I ran scans, and he came back as nothing. That should have raised red flags, but almost a week without sleep had exhausted me. Not thinking it through, I let him into the ship, and he immediately tore my arm off with his bare hands. If the dropship hadn't expulsed him, overriding my override, I'd be dead.

Still, the thing—the Quuin—had managed to destroy the food supplies. In its short time inside, it had also sabotaged the neural core—for all intents and purposes killing the ship. So, it was down to one option. There was some kind of station about eight hundred clicks to the east of our crash zone. I had no idea who ran it, why it was there, or if it even was a station at all.

I finished my bar. There was nothing else do but leave.

I pressed my remaining fingers into the weapons systems, felt them split. The display sprang up in front of me. I configured a battlesuit, pulling in the few microsynthesizers that had survived the journey. Grafted in the dropship's neurocortex. It made the suit unwieldy, but, assuming I was fortunate, the cortex might be able to plot a course home, if I could reconstruct Saowalak's neural handshake.

Here, I hesitated. Weapons, weapons. Heat seemed to work best. Projectiles did nothing. I loaded a thermal launcher, radiator panel, and a couple fission bombs. After a moment, I added a plasma lance, although I hadn't tested that one's effectiveness.

Okay, that should be good.

I pressed execute, and the acceleration gel molded itself to my body, pushing into the stump of my arm. I felt tendrils of the gel shove into my bicep, tapping into my brachial plexus. It hurt like crazy, but at least I'd have bimanual control of the battlesuit. I initiated another subroutine, and the dropship cockpit blossomed outward into plated fragments. Articulated pieces hissed out of manufacturing pods, weaving around the cockpit and locking into place around me. Layer upon layer, it built up until a vague egg shape encased me.

The acceleration gel prevented the shock from crushing me as the dropship ejected the battlesuit, discharging me through her belly. Two weapons arms, two manipulators, and two legs slammed on as I fell, spinning, landing upright on the sand below.

Hi, Saowalak. Quuin. Whatever you are. I'm ready for you.

He heard me fall and came running. I could sense the Quuin behind him somehow, a giant malignant shadow, just out of view.

I engaged the suit, running straight at him out from underneath the dropship. Saowalak's mouth was moving, talking. Curiosity got the better of me. I flipped acoustics on.

Saowalak's voice flooded into my brain. "I see you Gaan target arget arget ants ants. Command, I'm butcher block green..."

I clicked off acoustics. Same babble as before. I scrambled forward, running towards him as I charged the radiator panel. At ten yards, I pulsed it. Heat spread out, turning everything in front of me to glass.

Saowalak still was coming, but he was missing part of his face. And his sternum.

Looks human underneath.

I fired another pulse, three-second duration. When the heatwave cleared, I couldn't see anything. I kept running. Power was dipping low, the photovoltaic skin of the battlesuit was barely keeping up. Couldn't afford many more blasts like that.

I modified the legs' grip on the sand and saw a 10 MPH speed increase.

Good.

The battlesuit careened past the molten pit where Saowalak had stood and headed for the open desert.

Endless sand dunes spread ahead of me. Somewhere out there lay my salvation. I had to believe it was there. The exhaustion was overwhelming. I refused to sleep, but set the autoroute and let the suit do the work.

Ten miles out, the thing hit. I must have fallen asleep despite myself, or concussed when it knocked me down. I don't remember it coming.

I woke up to the suit face-down in a dune. I could hear a thousand maddening screeches on the suit's skin, like a grinder made of cat's teeth trying to bore through everywhere at once.

I gripped the suit's controls, trying to force it upright. No response. Tried again, transferring power. No response. Pulled up diagnostics. Everything checked green across the board.

Okay. Okay. Think.

My vision swam: I felt like puking. A ping on my display called my attention, and I pulled it in front of me, squinted.

Hemoglobin down to three. Platelets down to four thousand.

I'm bleeding to death, and I'm not clotting anymore. Wonderful. Think think think. THINK, Gan.

The tearing sound coming from outside was getting to me. Or maybe it was lack of perfusion to my brain. Drugs could only take my body so far.

Take my body so far ... but what about my mind?

I threw up.

Not much time left. I accessed the dropship's cortex, activating it. It sucked an enormous amount of power, but it didn't matter anymore; the suit wasn't taking me anywhere. I shut down everything except the photovoltaics and the ship's brain. Slaved myself into it. Scripted a consciousness transfer, tapping into the route used to upgrade the ship's AI.

What if I just copy myself, and I still die here?
I blacked out.
<<read error>>
//STOP PLAYBACK//

"Jon? Jon, where are you!"

"Down here, under the suit! Come on down. I found something."

"What are you doing down there? Never mind ... Is the ship coming?"

"Yeah, two minutes out. Clones are ready."

"You run the sim? How'd it check out?"

"Fine, except that when we actually do the consciousness transfer, we need to have full access to that huge brain that's slaved to the suit. Must have come from the dropship, huh? Wonder what he was doing with it."

"Never mind that now, Jon. I have to interface again, and I'm not waiting for the refractory period to be over. I need to hear from him."

<<throat clearing>>

"Listen, Gan. We're transferring you over into a clone, okay? I know about the thing in the sand. I saw it. I saw Saowalak. We have weapons on our ship that will obliterate whatever it is that's here with us. For now, I'm staying up here out of the sand, but you need to unlock the cortex so we can do the transfer. We can't transfer your actual consciousness without full access. You have to trust me."

<<fusion engines in the distance, closing rapidly>>

"There's the ship. I have time for one more. I'm going to try to get as close to your present time as I can. Our ship says it can brute force an insertion into a specific timeframe. Jon, hook me back in."

<<silence>>

"Jon? Hello??? Come on, man! Fine, I'll do it myself."

//BEGIN PLAYBACK//

If you're getting this, Lilli, I've unlocked the cortex. I'm ready for the transfer. STAY ON THE SUIT. Your companion Jon tried to attack you while you were last interfaced. I charged the skin, forced him off. The Quuin doesn't like electricity either ... figured that one out a while ago. The battlesuit will protect you, but I think when the Quuin consumed your friend, it damaged the suit somehow. Either way, it's staying off. I'm not getting enough data, though. Audio alone won't work for this. I need more. I'm trying something.

::video.start::

::success::

Holy nova. I've been entering the wrong script all these eons.

::access.eyelet1::

A heavy young man is staring at me, or, rather, at something that's on me. The sand around him is pulsing, shifting. Behind him, an angular craft comes to a hover over us.

Something pings my suit. The ship is calling me.

I complete the recognition handshake, binding myself to the ship's mainframe.

The heavy young man moves closer, reaches out, micrometers from touching my skin. Hesitates. I realize his eyes fixate on Lilli, who's on top of the suit, interfaced with my memory bank.

Don't.

He touches the skin. I wait for a discharge, but nothing happens. He smiles. It is a strange expression: stretching with a robotic symmetry beyond what is comfortable as though the person smiling can't sense the limits of the muscles. The corners of the mouth split, and blood trickles down.

Nonononono.

He starts climbing the suit. I dump all power into the skin, blasting electricity everywhere. The EMP's flare whites out my sensors. When they come back, he is still climbing. He disappears out of view, and I know he's reached her.

NONONONONONONONO. *Thinkthinkthinkthink. Come on, Gan!*

She's accessing you right now. The cortex is open, she's preparing transfer. Partition the cortex. MOVE, YOU IDIOT!

My mind is weak from so much disuse, but the old augments—even though they're now just virtual synthetics—kick into gear.

<<bone snapping>>

Not much time. I find her in the memory imaging unit. I'm sure she's totally unaware of what's happening right now. Interfacing causes complete dissociation.

Trace her back. There's the link. Inject a packet, watch it take off. The connection broadens. Still too small for realtime consciousness transfer, but time's something we're out of.

The connection winks, a millionth of a microsecond, but enough to let me know the connection is about to drop. The Quuin is killing her. Eating her, like it ate Saowalak.

I don't think about it anymore. I suck Lilli out of her brain, dumping her into the ship.

Above there is a flurry of activity, then silence.

A scraping sound, and the heavy man reappears on camera, this time looking directly into it.

At me.

His face is covered in blood. He turns his back, facing the ship. Watches it hovering for a moment.

The ship starts moving, coming in for a landing. The heavy man walks away to meet it. Around him, the sand is at a full boil, popping and bursting everywhere.

He's leaving the planet. The God help me.

I break the cortex's partition.

--Wha... where am ... WHATISGOINGON? WHATH-APPENED?--

I do a datadump, bringing her up to speed in the time it takes the ship to land. Easiest way to tell someone they're dead.

--It's taking the ship! We'll be trapped here! How can it even access the controls?--

Neural mimic, Lilli. Your friend Jon was gone most of the time you were here. I think the Quuin refrained from consuming you out of hopes you'd expose me to it. But now it's found something better. A whole ship, and a way off the planet.

We both watch as he boards the craft. The ship's engines flare. Preflight check.

--No...--

Listen, can you still access the clones through here? There's two, remember? We can still get out of here.

--I don't know...how...how do I access the ship?--

I graft a communications operator module onto her.

The ship begins to lift.

Hurry.

--I got it. Hang on. Accessing the ship.--

The ship pauses, a giant jewel dangling in midair.

--I froze acceleration, but he's overriding it. No matter, I'm in the genetics bay. Found the clones.--

The ship lifts skyward again. Out of its belly, a small panel unfolds and rotates towards us.

--Okay, ship's painting us with a broadbeam connection. Here goes nothing, Gan. I primed and modded the clones. The Quuin is going to have a tough time consuming them. There's also a weapons bay just down the hall and to the left from genetics. All kinds of nasty stuff in there. Guarantee, if we make it, we can wipe out whatever that thing is.

Got it. Weapons bay.

--*Starting the transfer. This will hurt. You will be completely disoriented when you wake up in your new body. Remember, head for the weapons bay.*--

--*See you up there, Gan.*--

See you up there, Lilli.

//STOP PLAYBACK//

ABOUT THE AUTHOR

Eric Kramer is a CRNA (nurse anesthetist) and a Family Nurse Practitioner. He lives in the rural Sierra Madre mountain range of northern Mexico with his wife and kids, serving the indigenous Tarahumara people group at a missions hospital with Mexico Medical Missions, providing anesthesia, primary care, and trauma services. You can find out more at mexicomedical.org. This is his second book.

www.ingramcontent.com/pod-product-compliance
Lightning Source LLC
Chambersburg PA
CBHW070332130626
46556CB00007B/2826